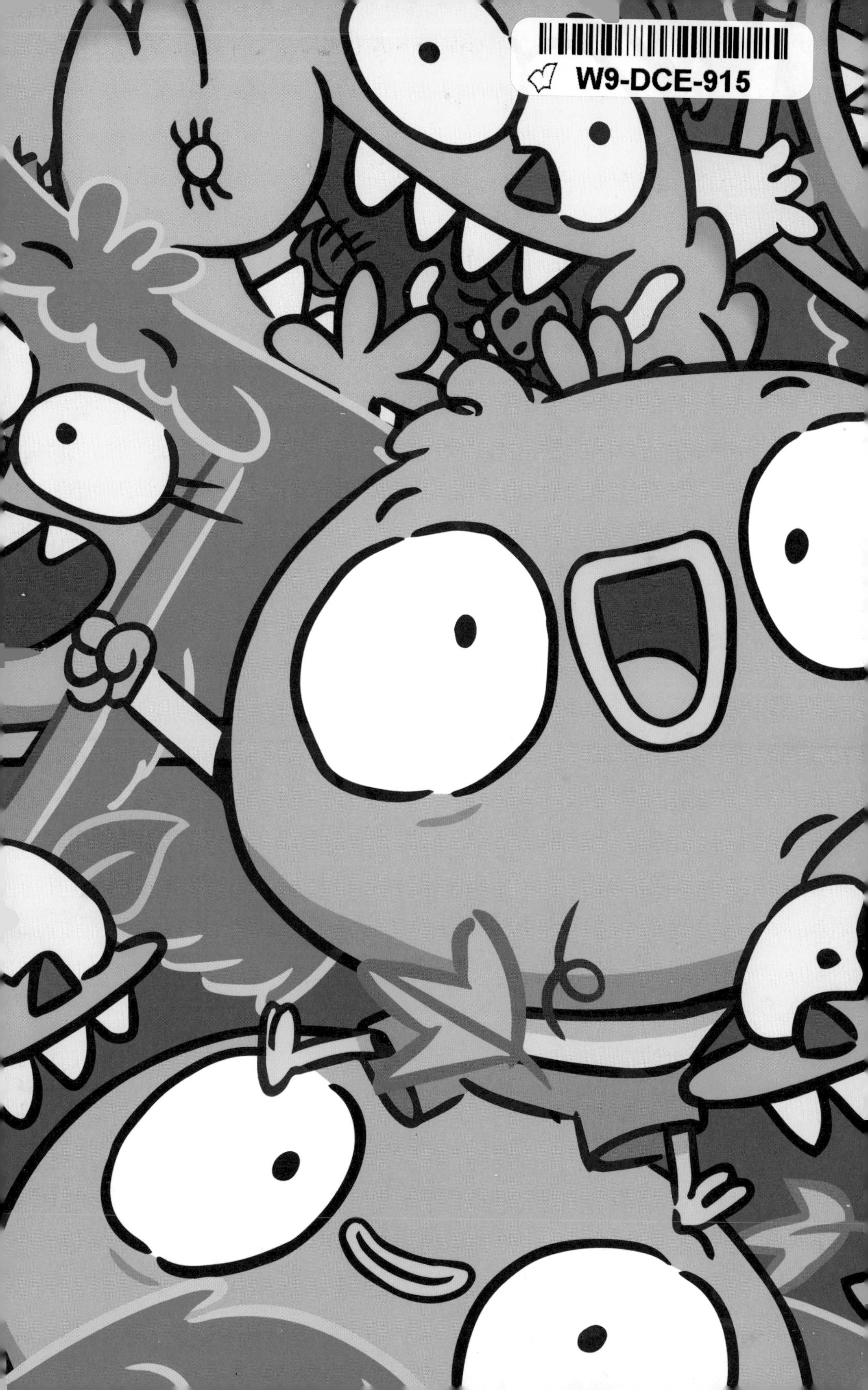

HARVEY BEAKS™

PAPERCUTZ™
NEW YORK

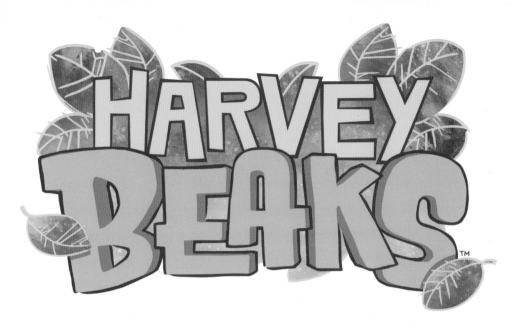

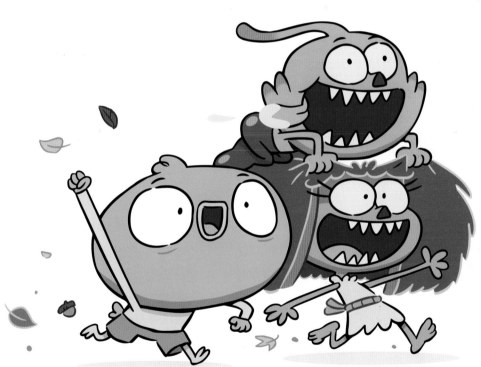

COMING SOON!

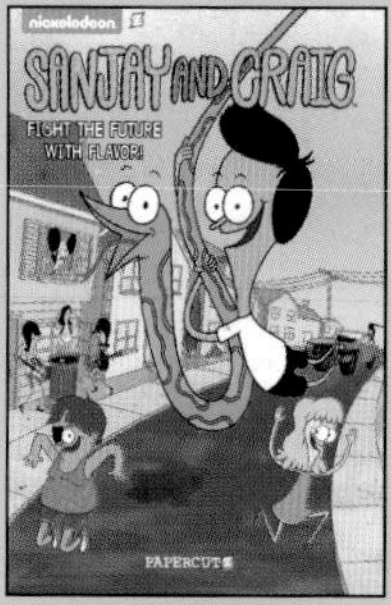
nickelodeon
SANJAY AND CRAIG
FIGHT THE FUTURE WITH FLAVOR!
PAPERCUTZ

#1 "Fight the Future with Flavor"

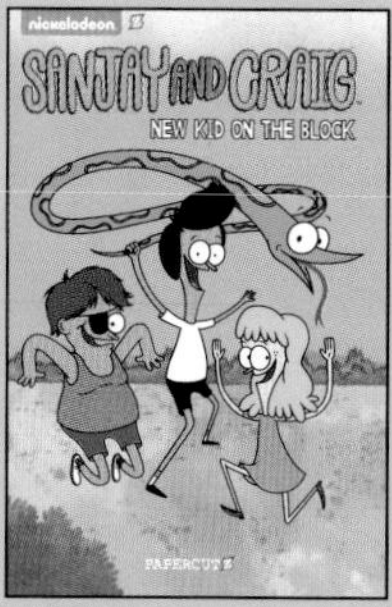
nickelodeon
SANJAY AND CRAIG
NEW KID ON THE BLOCK
PAPERCUTZ

#2 "New Kid on the Block"

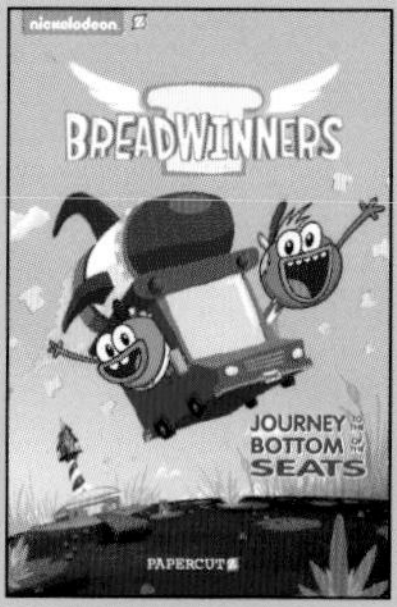
nickelodeon
BREADWINNERS
JOURNEY TO THE BOTTOM OF THE SEATS
PAPERCUTZ

#1 "Journey to the Bottom of the Seats"

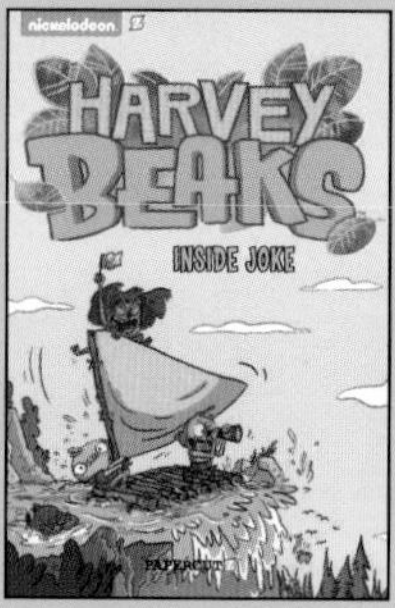
nickelodeon
HARVEY BEAKS
INSIDE JOKE
PAPERCUTZ

#1 "Inside Joke"

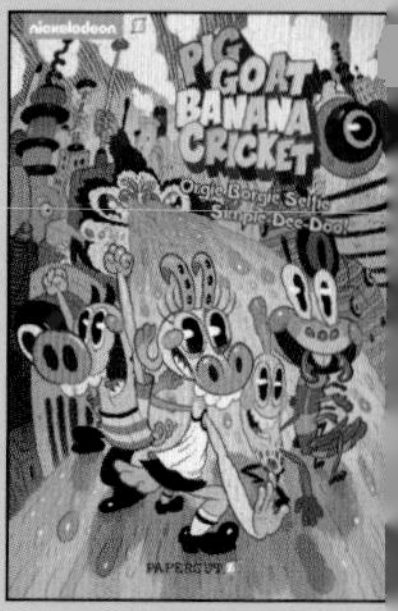
nickelodeon
PIG GOAT BANANA CRICKET
Orgle Borgle Selfie Simple-Dee-Doo!
PAPERCUTZ

#1 "Orgle Borgle Selfie Simple-Dee-Doo!"

Nickelodeon graphic novels are available for $7.99 in paperback, $12.99 in hardcover. Available from booksellers everywhere. You can also order online from Papercutz.com, or call 1-800-886-1223, Monday through Friday, 9-5 EST. MC, Visa, and AmEx accepted. To order by mail, please add $4.00 for postage and handling for first book ordered, $1.00 for each additional book and make check payable to NBM Publishing.
Send to: Papercutz, 160 Broadway, Suite 700, East Wing, New York, NY 10038.

Nickelodeon graphic novels are also available digitally wherever e-books are sold.

SUBSCRIBE!

The Greatest Kids Magazine in the world is here and you can be a charter subscriber. Be the first to get your copies and make sure you don't miss a single issue of the all-new Nickelodeon Magazine!

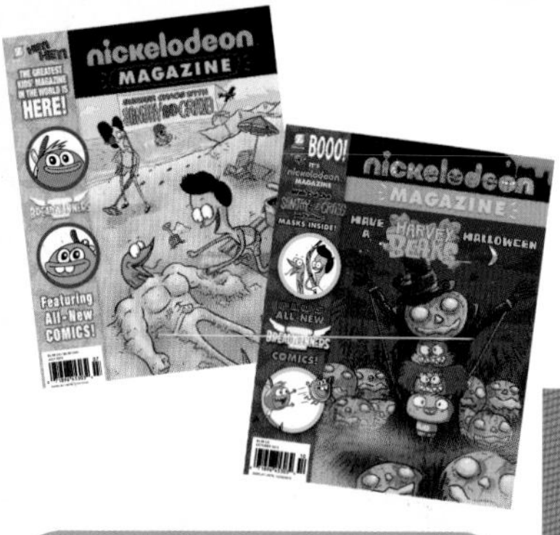
nickelodeon MAGAZINE
HERE!
Featuring All-New COMICS!
BOOO!
nickelodeon MAGAZINE
HARVEY BEAKS
HALLOWEEN
ALL NEW
COMICS!

Never miss an issue of nickelodeon™ MAGAZINE

Get Your Copies Delivered Right to Your Mailbox at Home!

Save! And Get Free Issues!

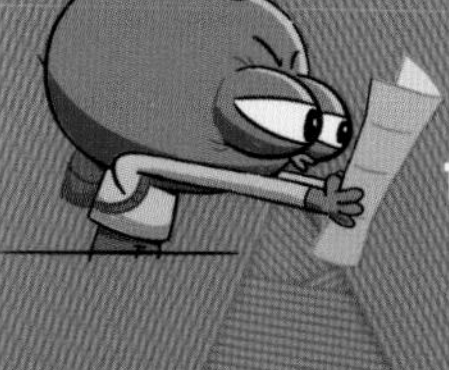

7 ISSUES FOR THE PRICE OF 6!

+SAVE $7 OFF COVER PRICE!

6 REGULAR ISSUES
+1 BONUS FREE ISSUE
7 ISSUES FOR ONLY $27.50

14 ISSUES FOR THE PRICE OF 12!

+SAVE $14 OFF COVER PRICE!

12 REGULAR ISSUES
+2 BONUS FREE ISSUES
14 ISSUES FOR ONLY $49.99

DIGITAL SUBSCRIPTION - ONLY $19.99 - OR FREE FOR ALL PRINT SUBSCRIBERS!

ORDER ONLINE at Papercutz.com/nickmag

OR CALL 1-800-778-6278

(Please have debit/credit card ready)

Use promo code: HBGN1.

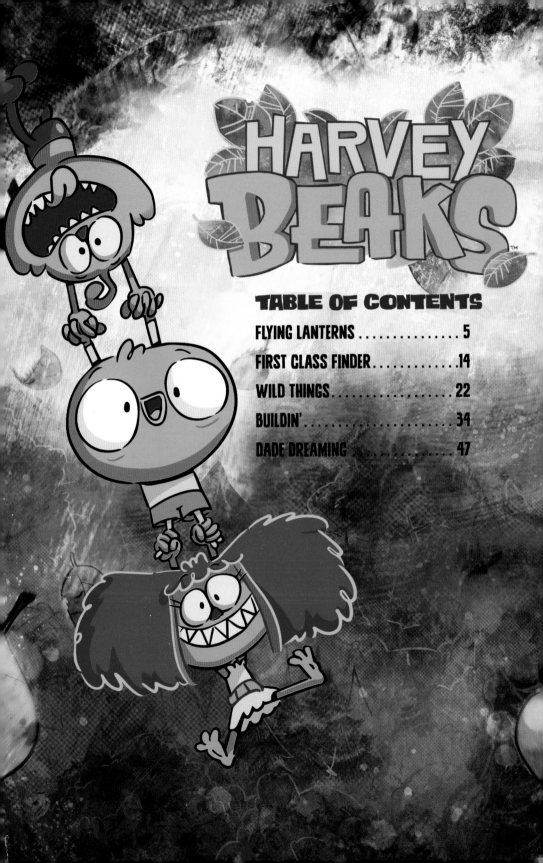

TABLE OF CONTENTS

FLYING LANTERNS 5

FIRST CLASS FINDER 14

WILD THINGS 22

BUILDIN' 34

DADE DREAMING 47

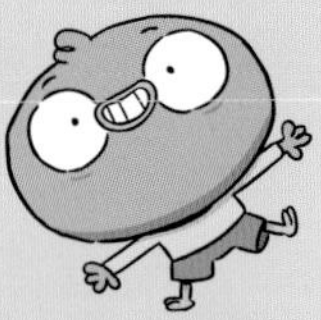

HARVEY BEAKS

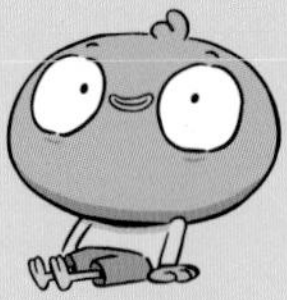

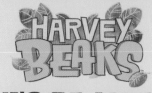

INSIDE JOKE

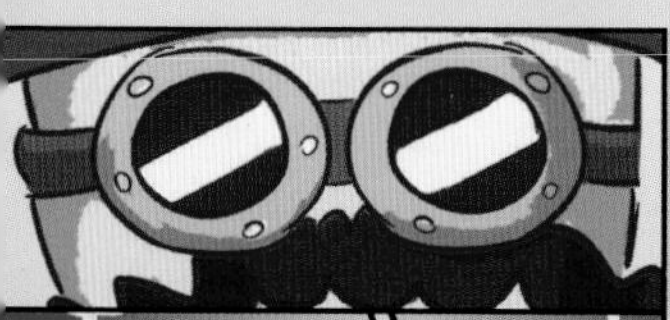
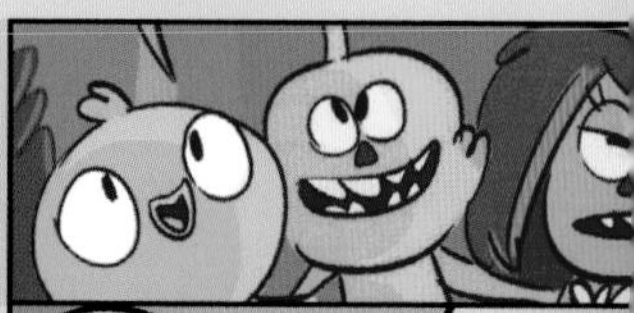

"FLYING LANTERNS"
STEFAN PETRUCHA AND
THE HARVEY BEAKS SHOW WRITERS - WRITERS
ANDREAS SCHUSTER - ARTIST, LETTERER, AND COLORIST

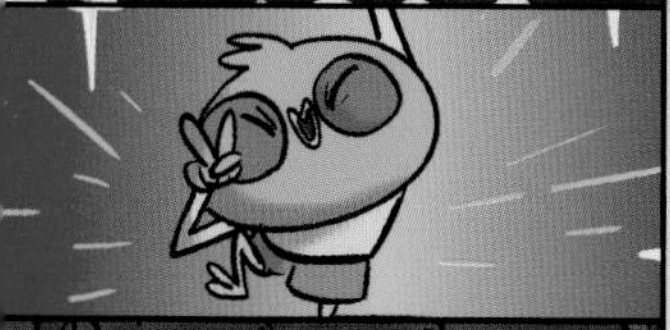
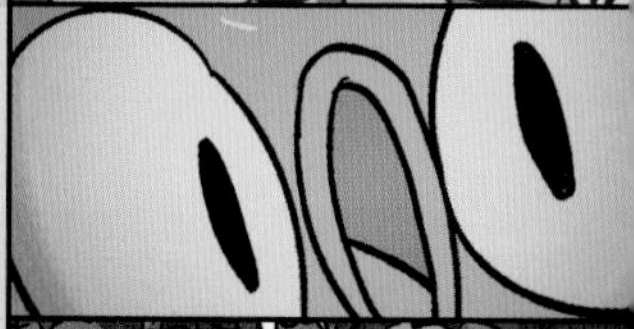

"FIRST CLASS FINDER"
STEFAN PETRUCHA AND
THE HARVEY BEAKS SHOW WRITERS - WRITERS
ANDREAS SCHUSTER - ARTIST & LETTERER
LAURIE E. SMITH - COLORIST

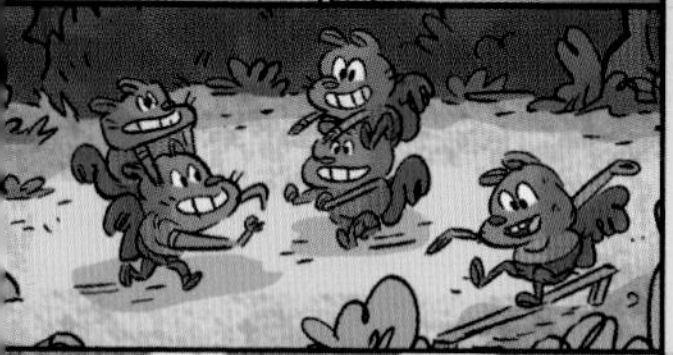
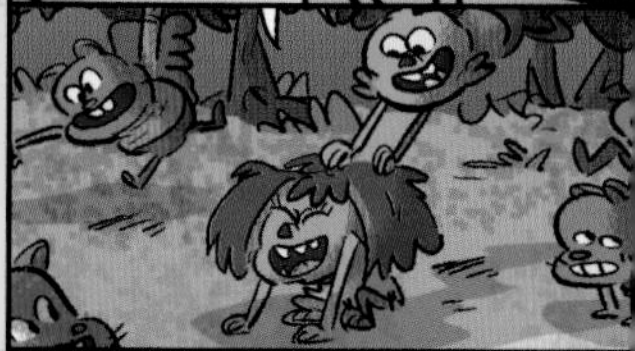

"WILD THINGS"
STEFAN PETRUCHA- WRITER
ANDREAS SCHUSTER - ARTIST & LETTERER
LAURIE E. SMITH - COLORIST

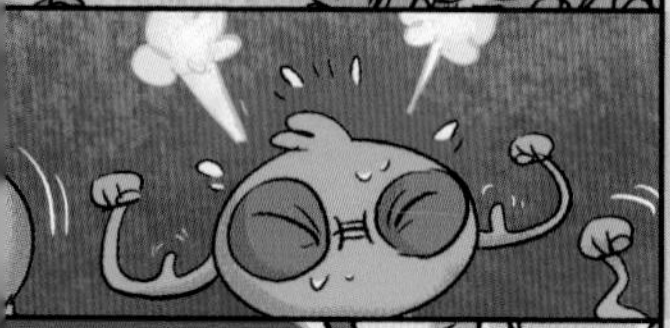
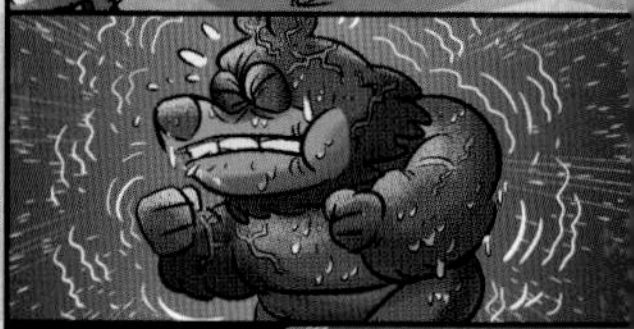

"BUILDIN'"
CARSON MONTGOMERY - WRITER
ANDREAS SCHUSTER - ARTIST & LETTERER
LAURIE E. SMITH - COLORIST

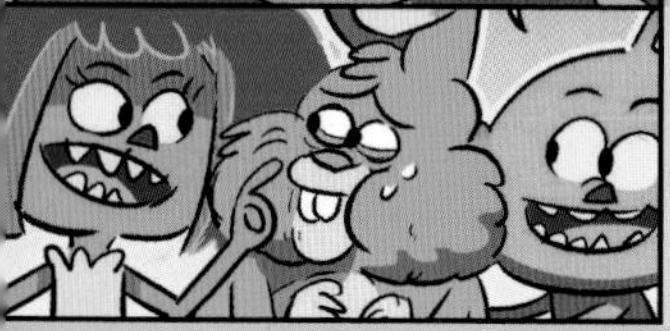
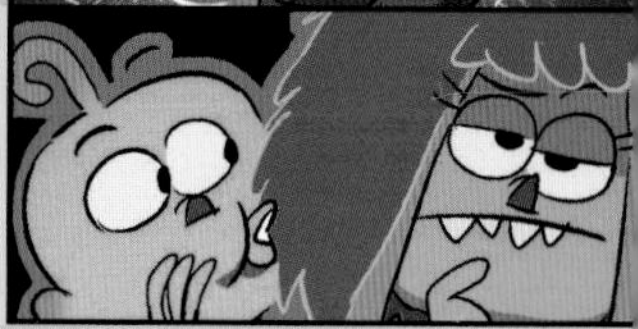

"DADE DREAMING"
SHANE HOUGHTON, WRITER
ANDREAS SCHUSTER - ARTIST & LETTERER
MATT HERMS - COLORIST

BASED ON THE NICKELODEON ANIMATED TV SERIES CREATED BY C.H. GREENBLATT

JAMES SALERNO - SR. ART DIRECTOR/NICKELODEON
CHRIS NELSON - DESIGN/PRODUCTION
JEFF WHITMAN - PRODUCTION COORDINATOR
BETHANY BRYAN - EDITOR
JOAN HILTY - COMICS EDITOR/NICKELODEON
ASANTE SIMONS - EDITORIAL INTERN
JIM SALICRUP
EDITOR-IN-CHIEF

ISBN: 978-1-62991-431-2 PAPERBACK EDITION
ISBN: 978-1-62991-432-9 HARDCOVER EDITION

PAPERCUTZ BOOKS MAY BE PURCHASED FOR BUSINESS OR PROMOTIONAL USE. FOR INFORMATION ON BULK PURCHASES PLEASE CONTACT MACMILLAN CORPORATE AND PREMIUM SALES DEPARTMENT AT (800) 221-7945 X5442.

PRINTED IN CHINA FEBRUARY 2016 BY IMAGO
2/F, BLK, 402, CAI DIAN INDUSTRIAL ZONE
HUANGGANG NORTH ROAD
FUTIAN DISTRICT, SHENZHEN
CHINA

DISTRIBUTED BY MACMILLAN
FIRST PRINTING

Thanks for visiting YDL today!

Whittaker Road Library
10/09/21 11:17AM

****

PATRON: ***********6110

****

Harvey Beaks : inside joke.
ygn
CALL NO: YOUTH GRAPHIC NOVEL Har
37101951213753   10/30/21

TOTAL: 1

Support YDL by shopping! Learn
more at ypsilibrary.org/donate.
Renew items on the YDL App, at
ypsilibrary.org, or 734.482.4110

HARVEY BEAKS

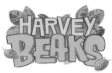

FLYING LANTERNS

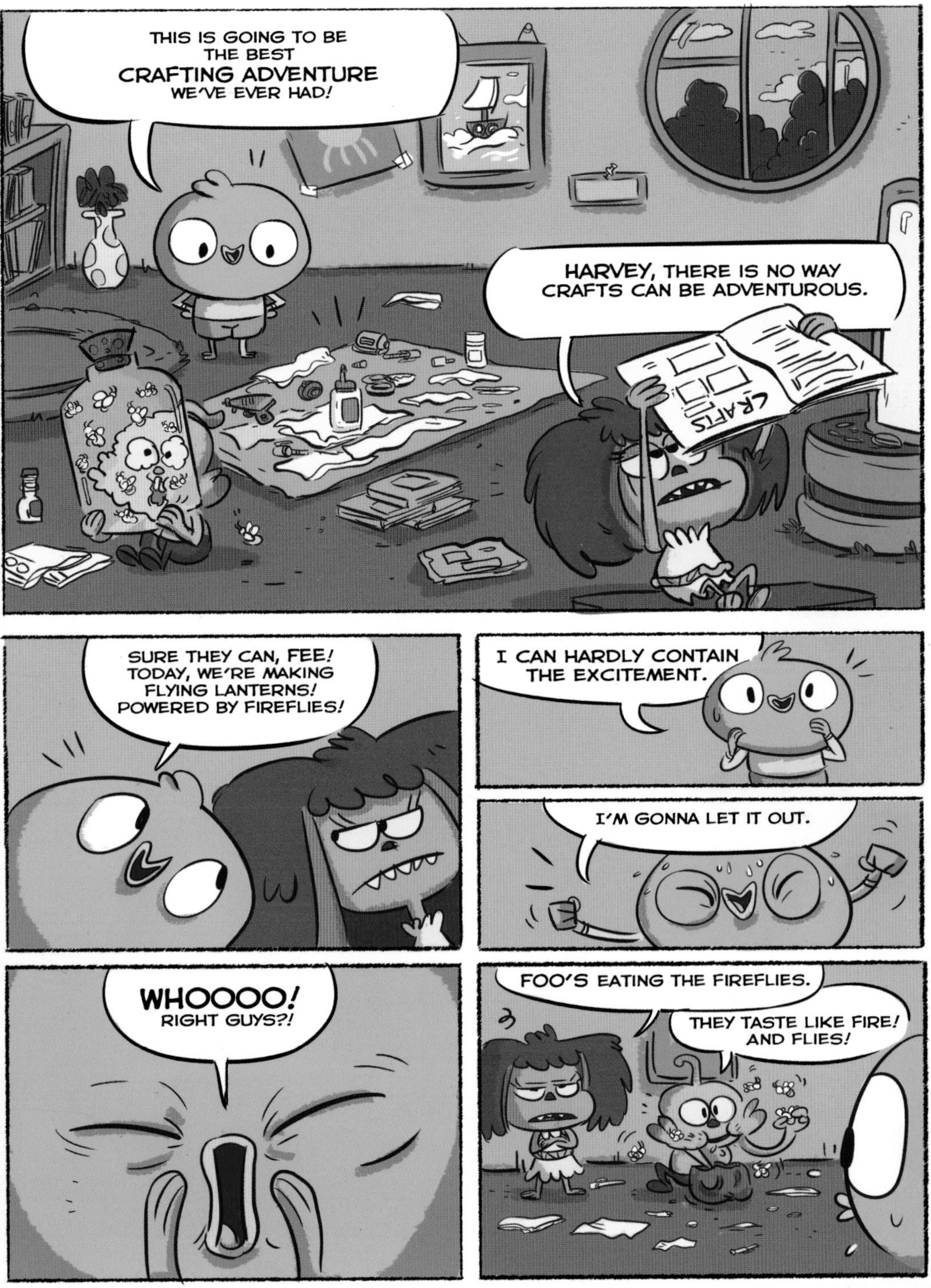
THIS IS GOING TO BE THE BEST CRAFTING ADVENTURE WE'VE EVER HAD!
HARVEY, THERE IS NO WAY CRAFTS CAN BE ADVENTUROUS.
CRAFTS
SURE THEY CAN, FEE! TODAY, WE'RE MAKING FLYING LANTERNS! POWERED BY FIREFLIES!
I CAN HARDLY CONTAIN THE EXCITEMENT.
I'M GONNA LET IT OUT.
WHOOOO! RIGHT GUYS?!
FOO'S EATING THE FIREFLIES.
THEY TASTE LIKE FIRE! AND FLIES!

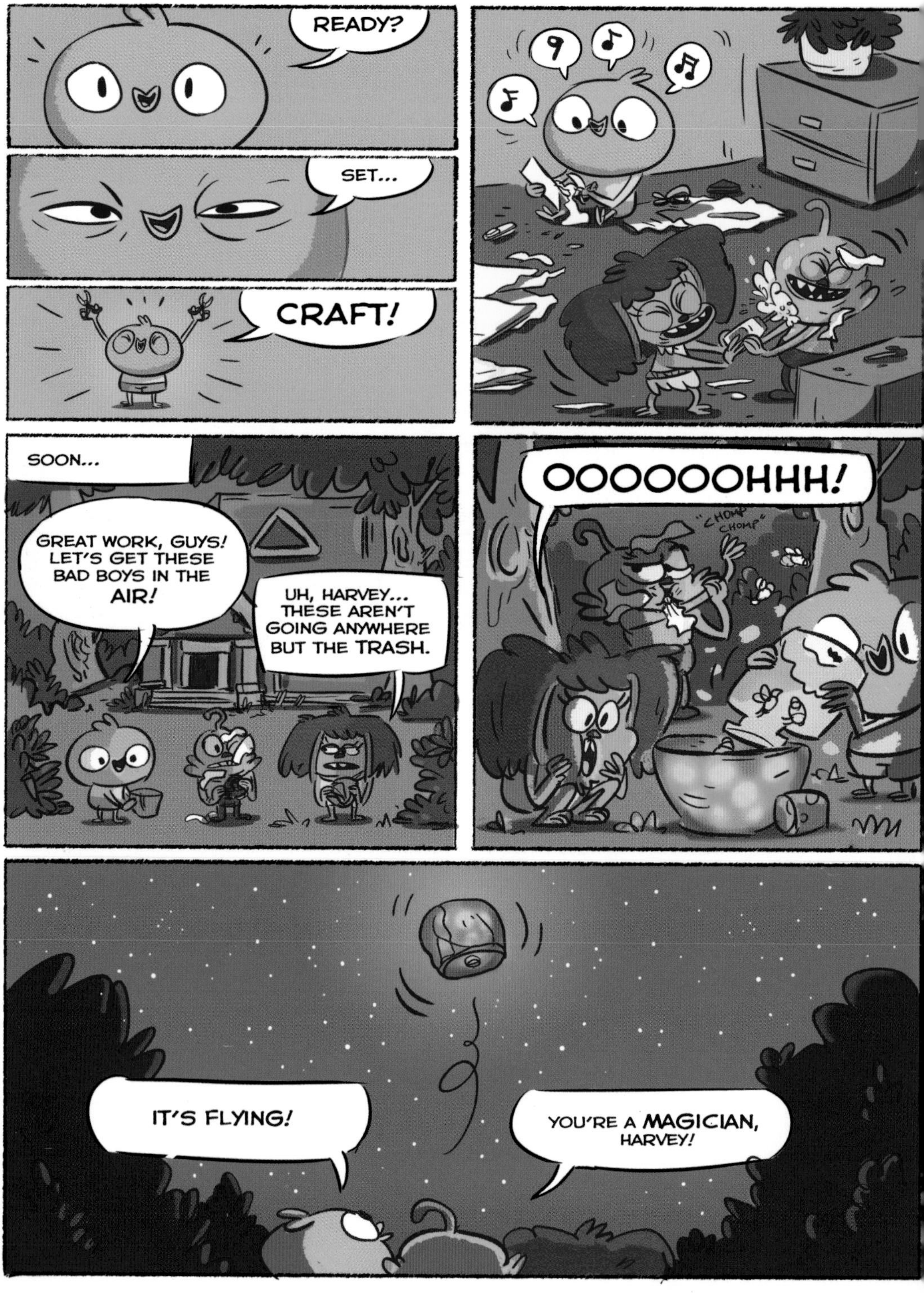
READY?
SET...
CRAFT!
SOON...
GREAT WORK, GUYS! LET'S GET THESE BAD BOYS IN THE AIR!
UH, HARVEY... THESE AREN'T GOING ANYWHERE BUT THE TRASH.
OOOOOOHHH!
"CHOMP CHOMP"
IT'S FLYING!
YOU'RE A MAGICIAN, HARVEY!

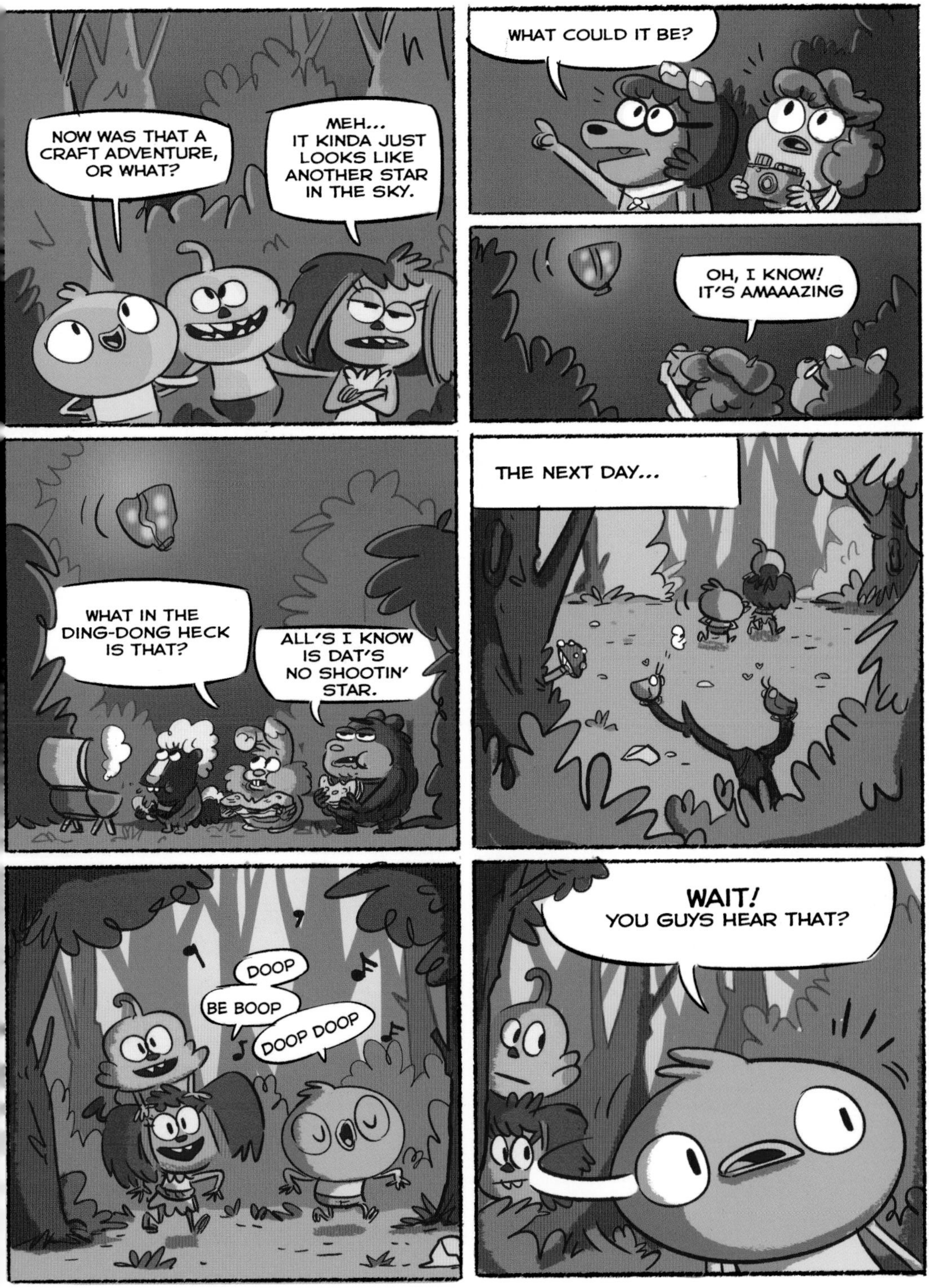
NOW WAS THAT A CRAFT ADVENTURE, OR WHAT?
MEH... IT KINDA JUST LOOKS LIKE ANOTHER STAR IN THE SKY.
WHAT COULD IT BE?
OH, I KNOW! IT'S AMAAAZING
WHAT IN THE DING-DONG HECK IS THAT?
ALL'S I KNOW IS DAT'S NO SHOOTIN' STAR.
THE NEXT DAY...
DOOP
BE BOOP
DOOP DOOP
WAIT! YOU GUYS HEAR THAT?

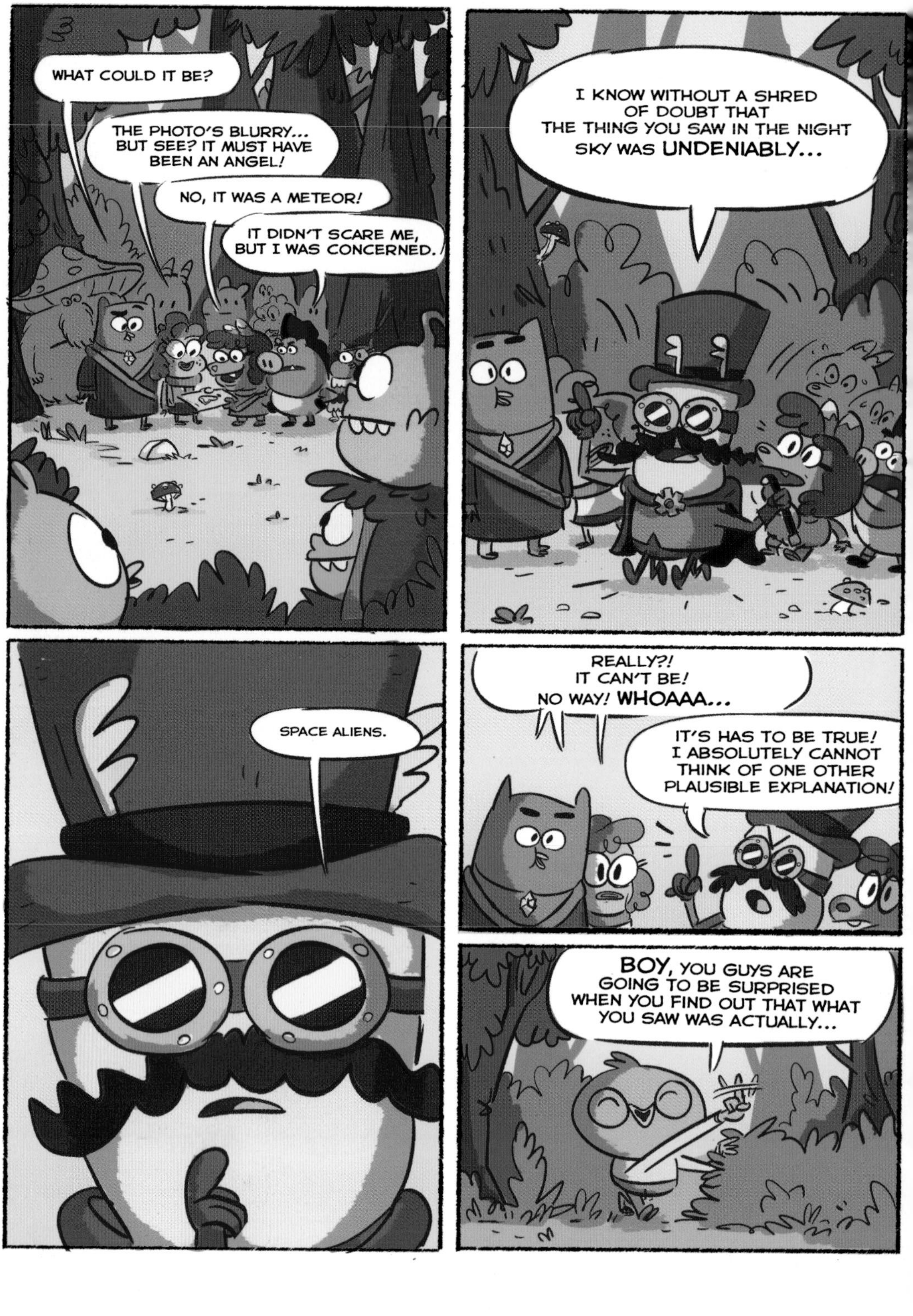
WHAT COULD IT BE?
THE PHOTO'S BLURRY... BUT SEE? IT MUST HAVE BEEN AN ANGEL!
NO, IT WAS A METEOR!
IT DIDN'T SCARE ME, BUT I WAS CONCERNED.
I KNOW WITHOUT A SHRED OF DOUBT THAT THE THING YOU SAW IN THE NIGHT SKY WAS UNDENIABLY...
SPACE ALIENS.
REALLY?! IT CAN'T BE! NO WAY! WHOAAA...
IT'S HAS TO BE TRUE! I ABSOLUTELY CANNOT THINK OF ONE OTHER PLAUSIBLE EXPLANATION!
BOY, YOU GUYS ARE GOING TO BE SURPRISED WHEN YOU FIND OUT THAT WHAT YOU SAW WAS ACTUALLY...

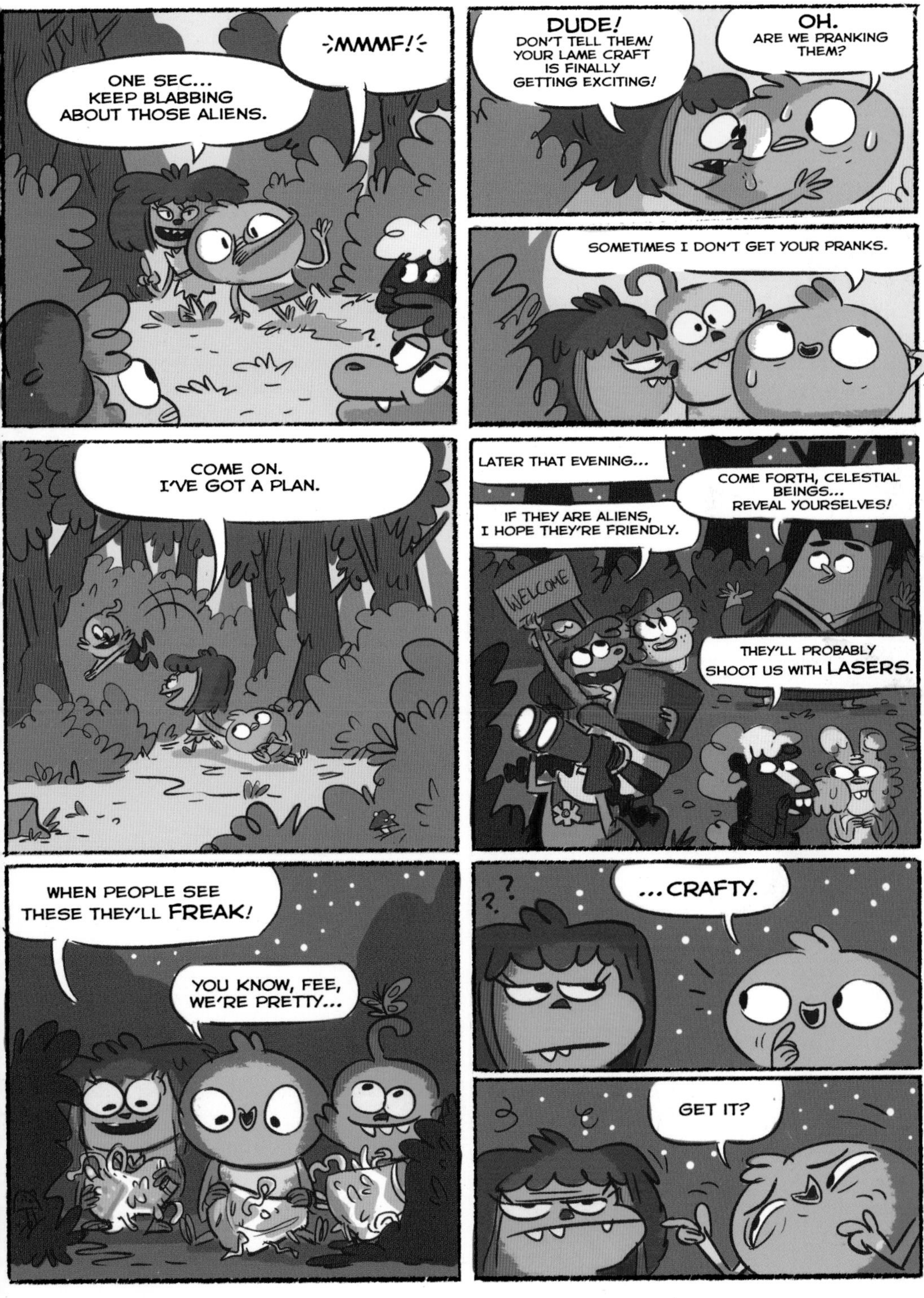
ONE SEC... KEEP BLABBING ABOUT THOSE ALIENS.
MMMF!
DUDE! DON'T TELL THEM! YOUR LAME CRAFT IS FINALLY GETTING EXCITING!
OH. ARE WE PRANKING THEM?
SOMETIMES I DON'T GET YOUR PRANKS.
COME ON. I'VE GOT A PLAN.
LATER THAT EVENING...
COME FORTH, CELESTIAL BEINGS... REVEAL YOURSELVES!
IF THEY ARE ALIENS, I HOPE THEY'RE FRIENDLY.
WELCOME
THEY'LL PROBABLY SHOOT US WITH LASERS.
WHEN PEOPLE SEE THESE THEY'LL FREAK!
YOU KNOW, FEE, WE'RE PRETTY...
...CRAFTY.
GET IT?

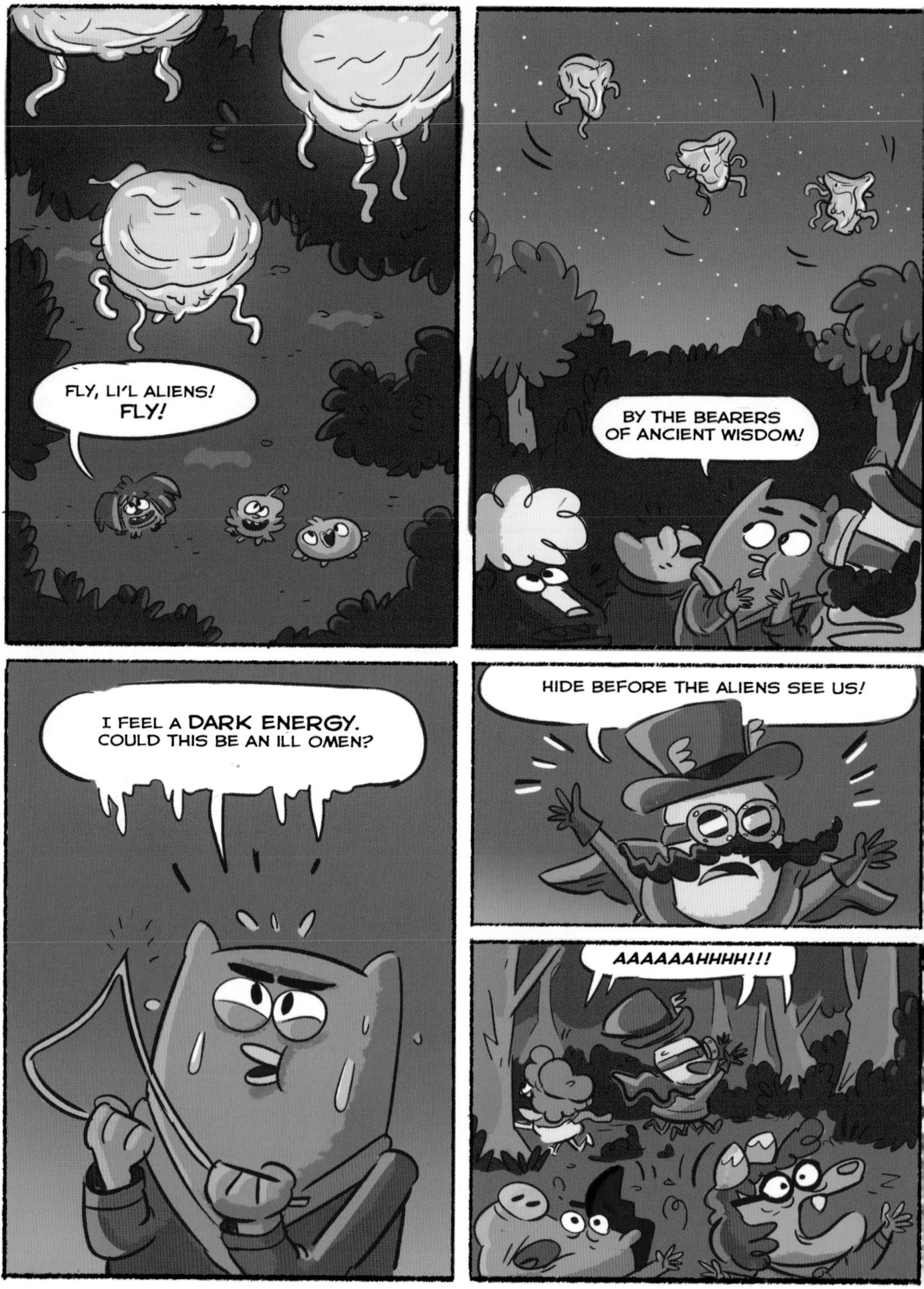
FLY, LI'L ALIENS! FLY!
BY THE BEARERS OF ANCIENT WISDOM!
I FEEL A DARK ENERGY. COULD THIS BE AN ILL OMEN?
HIDE BEFORE THE ALIENS SEE US!
AAAAAAHHHH!!!

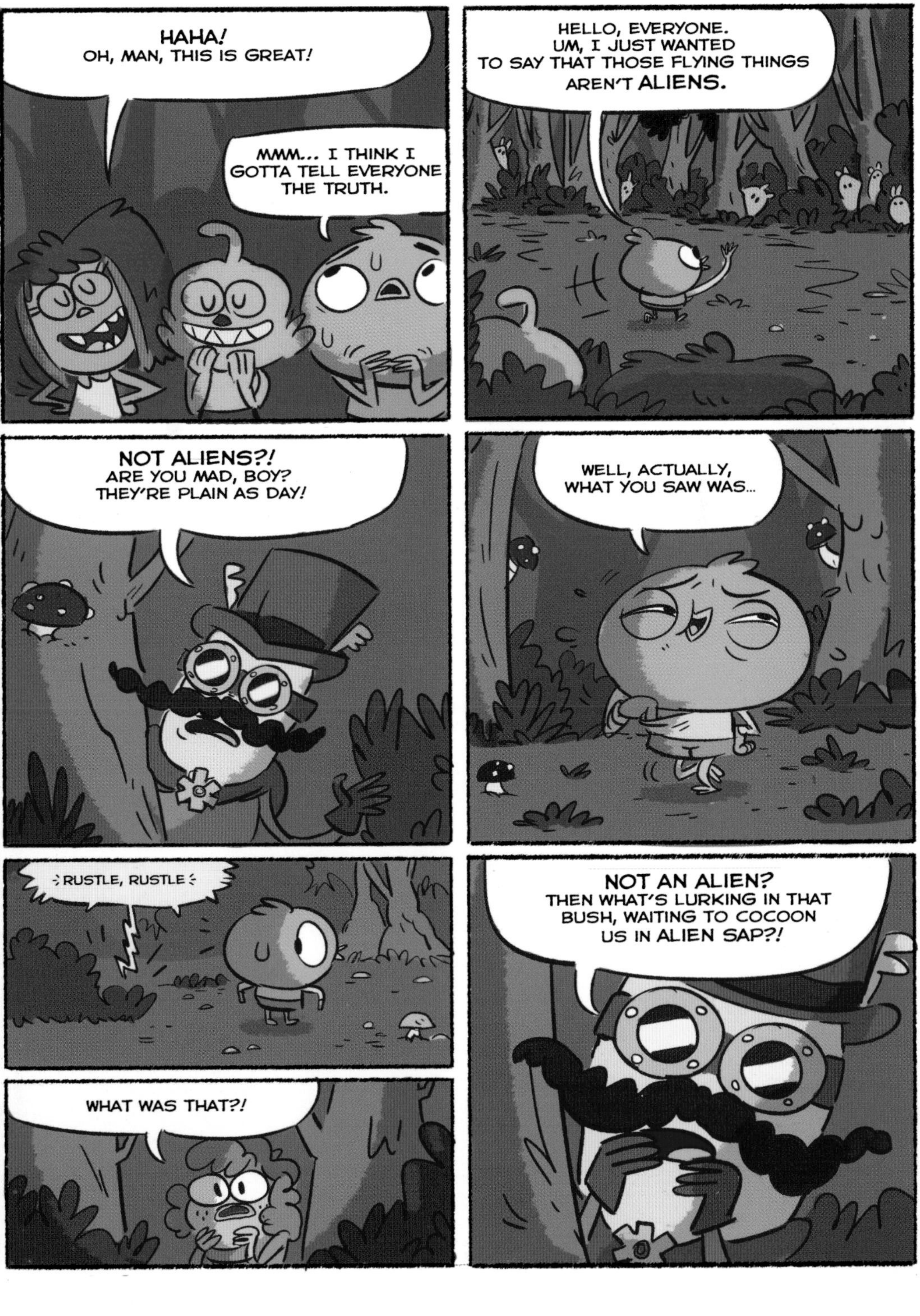
HAHA! OH, MAN, THIS IS GREAT!
MMM... I THINK I GOTTA TELL EVERYONE THE TRUTH.
HELLO, EVERYONE. UM, I JUST WANTED TO SAY THAT THOSE FLYING THINGS AREN'T ALIENS.
NOT ALIENS?! ARE YOU MAD, BOY? THEY'RE PLAIN AS DAY!
WELL, ACTUALLY, WHAT YOU SAW WAS...
RUSTLE, RUSTLE
WHAT WAS THAT?!
NOT AN ALIEN? THEN WHAT'S LURKING IN THAT BUSH, WAITING TO COCOON US IN ALIEN SAP?!

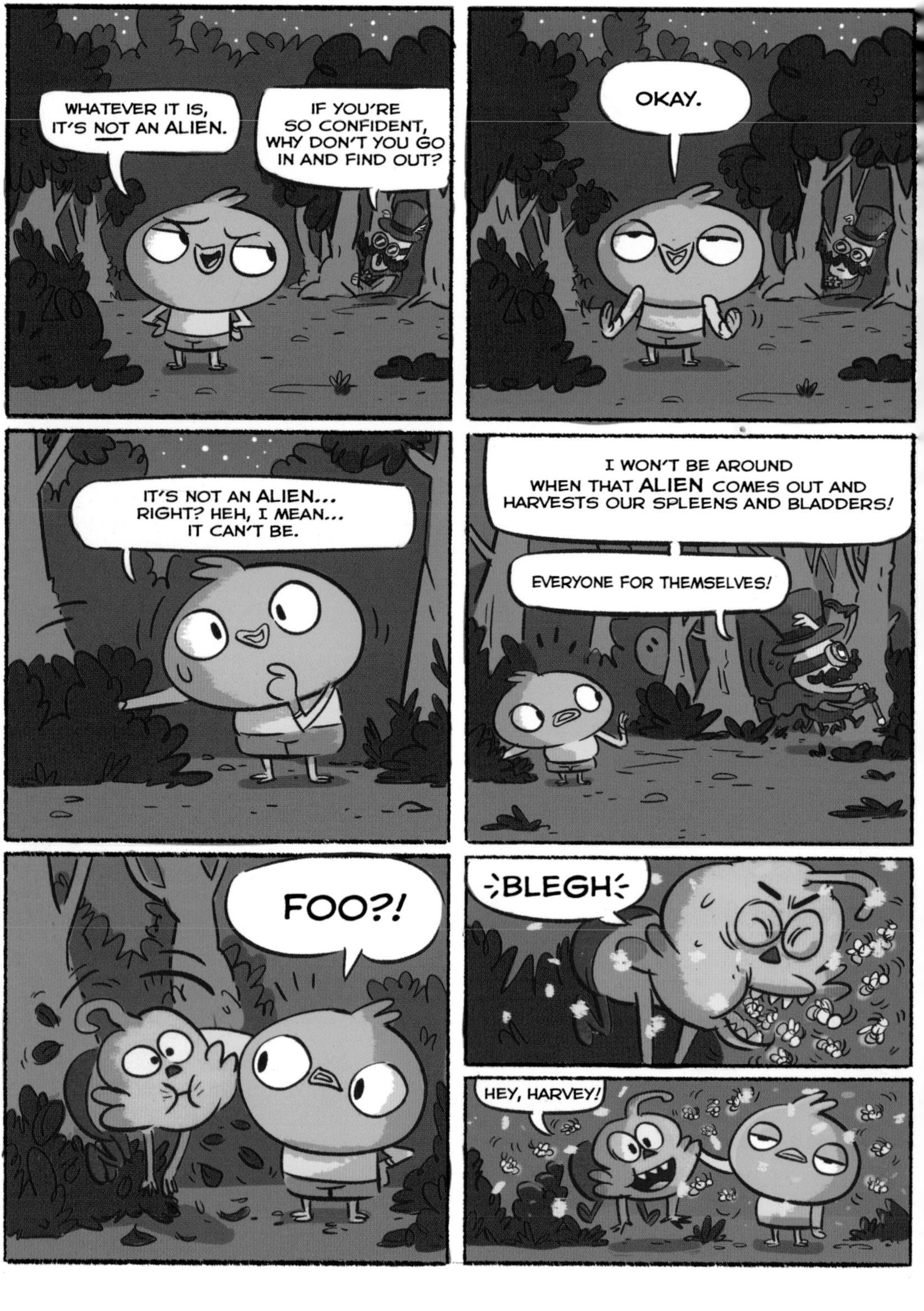
WHATEVER IT IS, IT'S NOT AN ALIEN.
IF YOU'RE SO CONFIDENT, WHY DON'T YOU GO IN AND FIND OUT?
OKAY.
IT'S NOT AN ALIEN... RIGHT? HEH, I MEAN... IT CAN'T BE.
I WON'T BE AROUND WHEN THAT ALIEN COMES OUT AND HARVESTS OUR SPLEENS AND BLADDERS!
EVERYONE FOR THEMSELVES!
FOO?!
BLEGH
HEY, HARVEY!

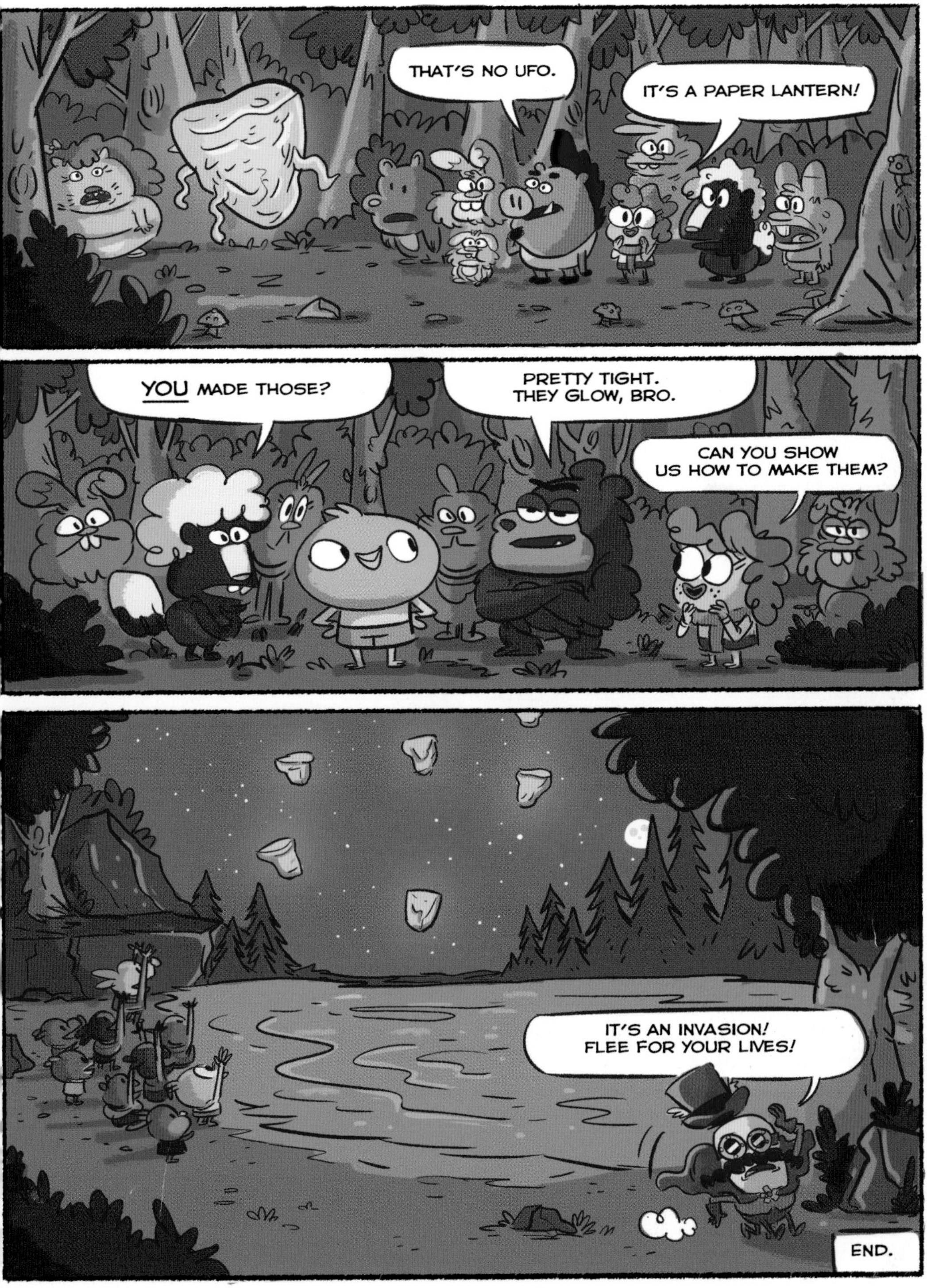
THAT'S NO UFO.
IT'S A PAPER LANTERN!
YOU MADE THOSE?
PRETTY TIGHT. THEY GLOW, BRO.
CAN YOU SHOW US HOW TO MAKE THEM?
IT'S AN INVASION! FLEE FOR YOUR LIVES!
END.

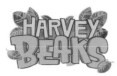

FIRST CLASS FINDER

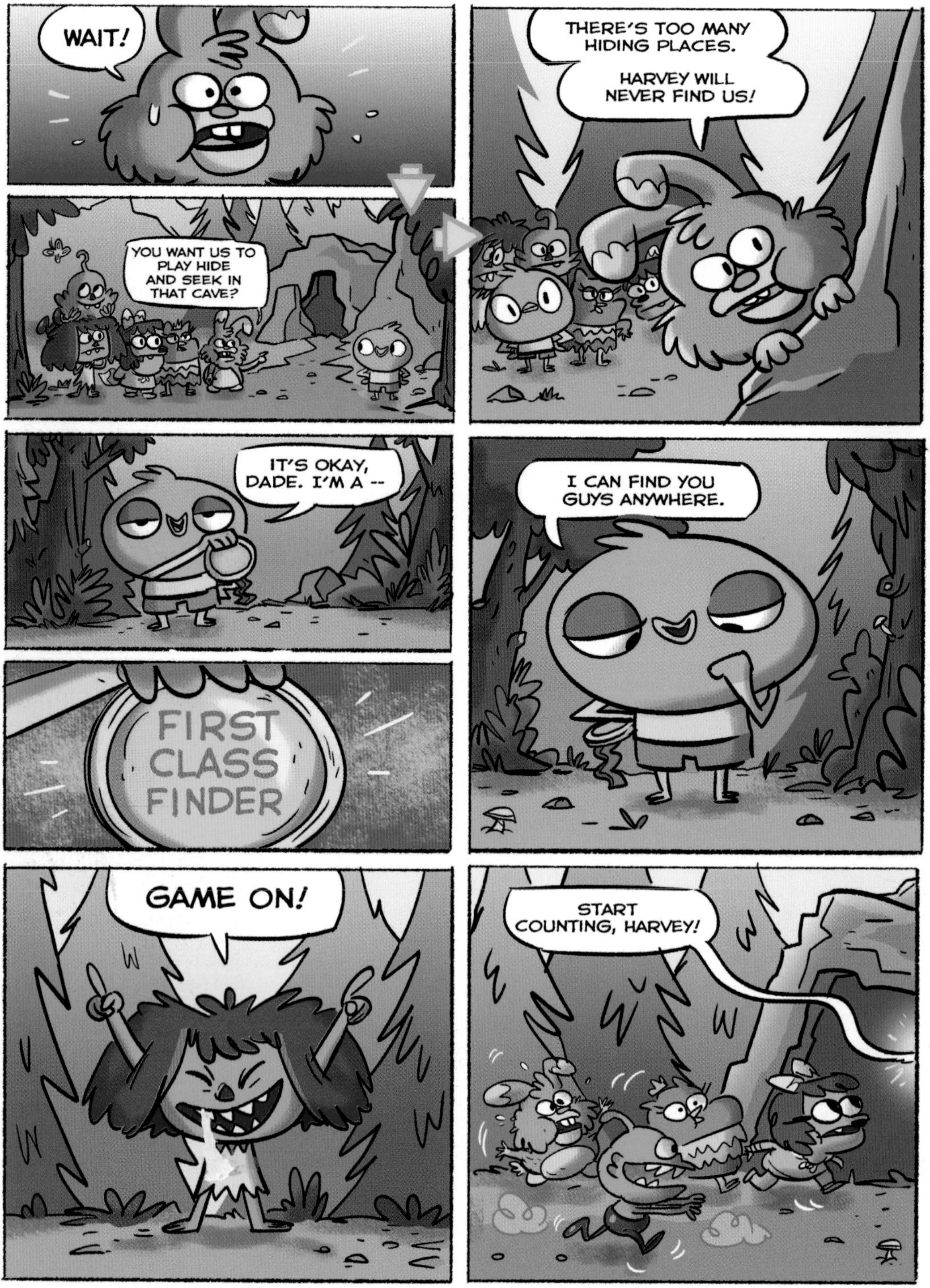

WAIT!
YOU WANT US TO PLAY HIDE AND SEEK IN THAT CAVE?
THERE'S TOO MANY HIDING PLACES.
HARVEY WILL NEVER FIND US!
IT'S OKAY, DADE. I'M A --
FIRST CLASS FINDER
I CAN FIND YOU GUYS ANYWHERE.
GAME ON!
START COUNTING, HARVEY!

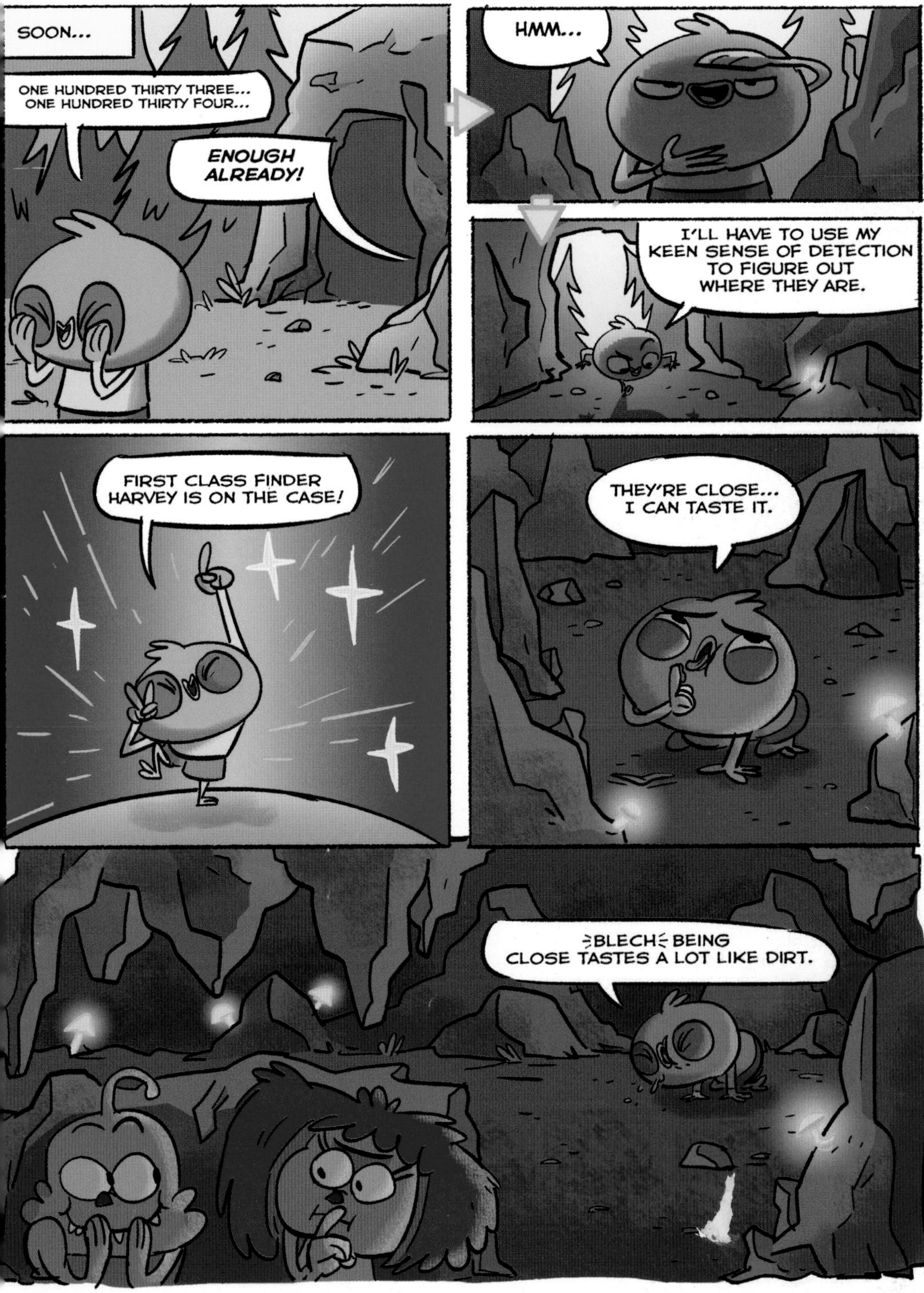
SOON...
ONE HUNDRED THIRTY THREE... ONE HUNDRED THIRTY FOUR...
ENOUGH ALREADY!
HMM...
I'LL HAVE TO USE MY KEEN SENSE OF DETECTION TO FIGURE OUT WHERE THEY ARE.
FIRST CLASS FINDER HARVEY IS ON THE CASE!
THEY'RE CLOSE... I CAN TASTE IT.
BLECH BEING CLOSE TASTES A LOT LIKE DIRT.

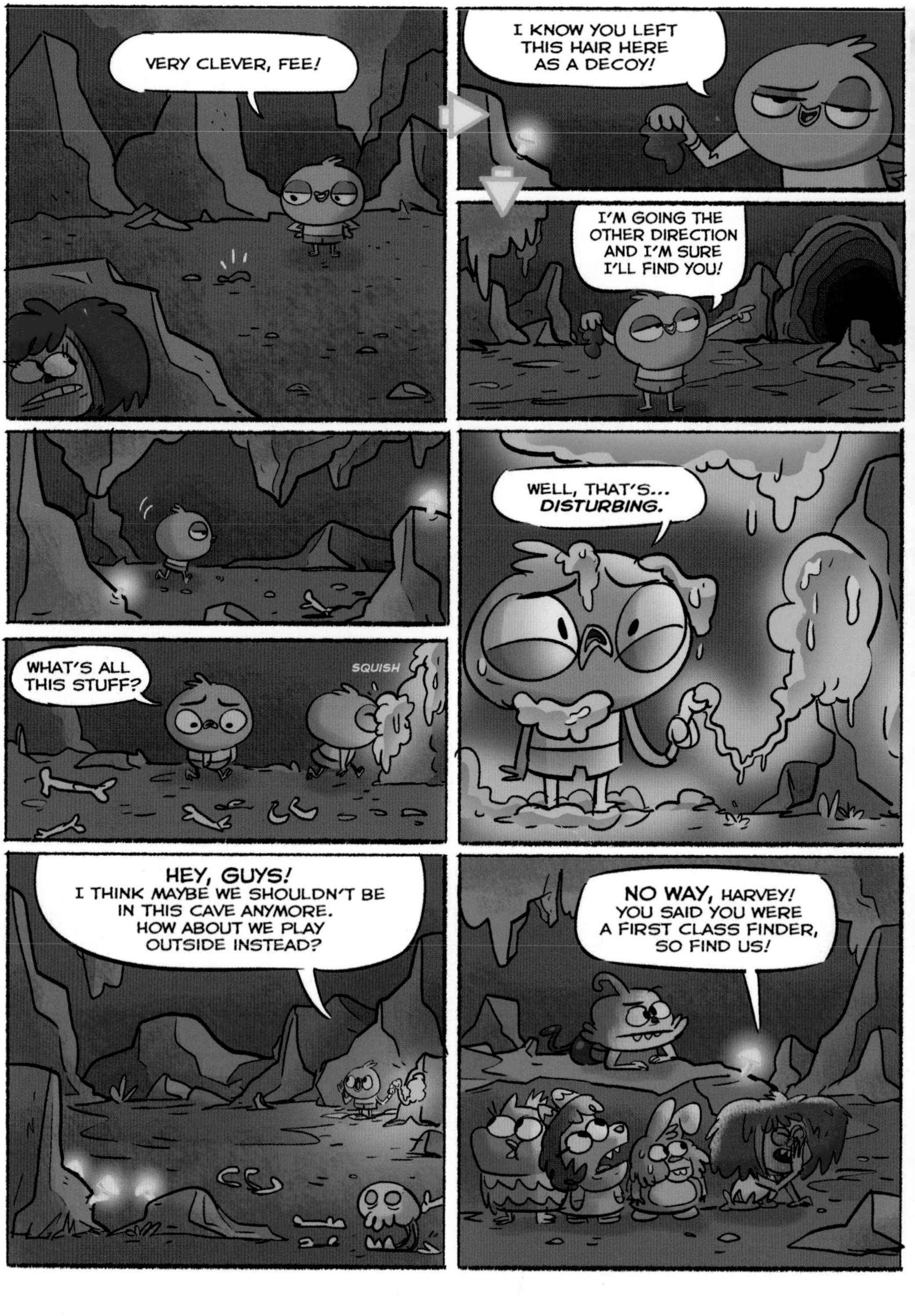
VERY CLEVER, FEE!
I KNOW YOU LEFT THIS HAIR HERE AS A DECOY!
I'M GOING THE OTHER DIRECTION AND I'M SURE I'LL FIND YOU!
WHAT'S ALL THIS STUFF?
SQUISH
WELL, THAT'S... DISTURBING.
HEY, GUYS! I THINK MAYBE WE SHOULDN'T BE IN THIS CAVE ANYMORE. HOW ABOUT WE PLAY OUTSIDE INSTEAD?
NO WAY, HARVEY! YOU SAID YOU WERE A FIRST CLASS FINDER, SO FIND US!

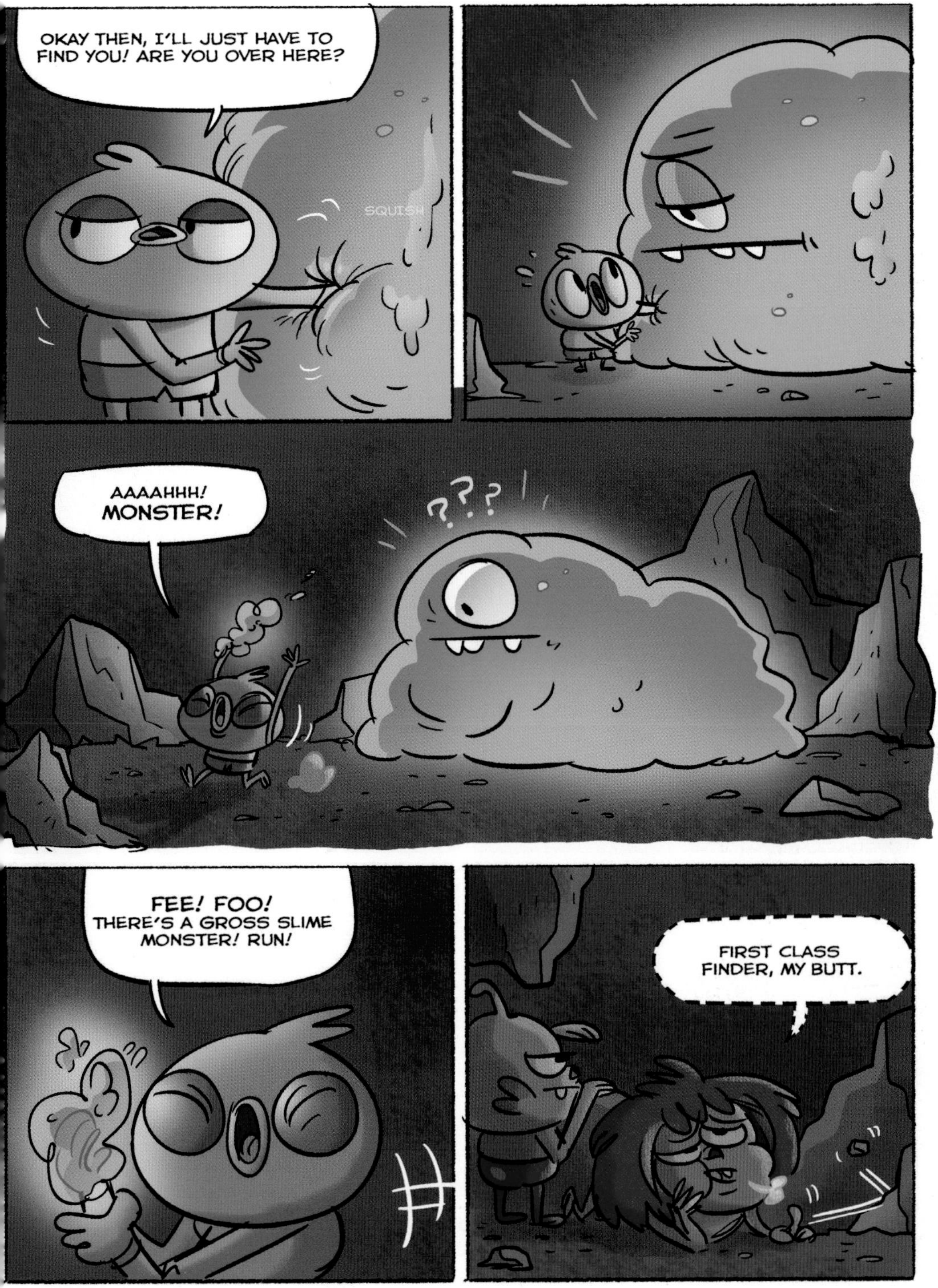
OKAY THEN, I'LL JUST HAVE TO FIND YOU! ARE YOU OVER HERE?
SQUISH
AAAAHHH! MONSTER!
???
FEE! FOO! THERE'S A GROSS SLIME MONSTER! RUN!
FIRST CLASS FINDER, MY BUTT.

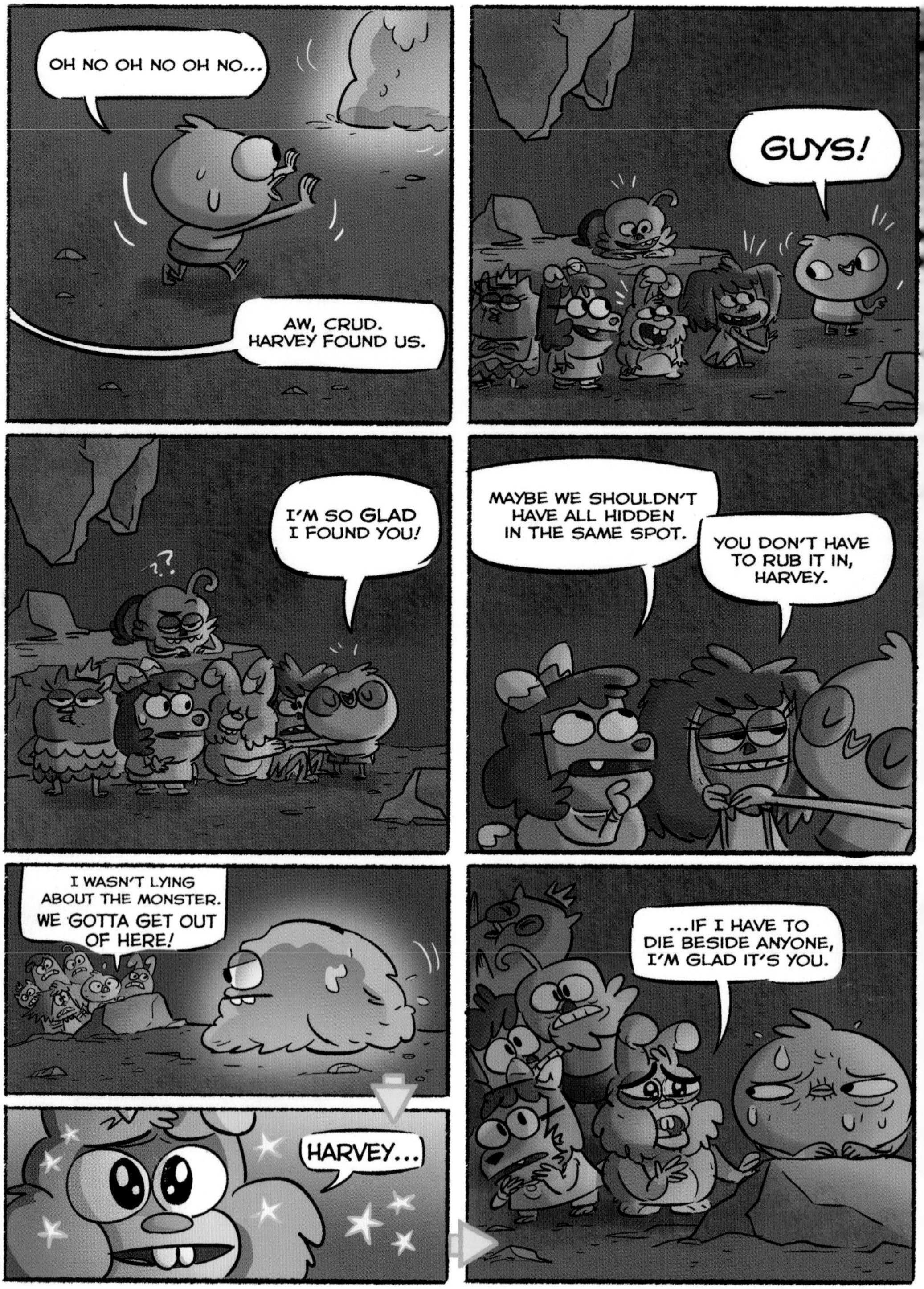
OH NO OH NO OH NO...
AW, CRUD. HARVEY FOUND US.
GUYS!
I'M SO GLAD I FOUND YOU!
MAYBE WE SHOULDN'T HAVE ALL HIDDEN IN THE SAME SPOT.
YOU DON'T HAVE TO RUB IT IN, HARVEY.
I WASN'T LYING ABOUT THE MONSTER. WE GOTTA GET OUT OF HERE!
HARVEY...
...IF I HAVE TO DIE BESIDE ANYONE, I'M GLAD IT'S YOU.

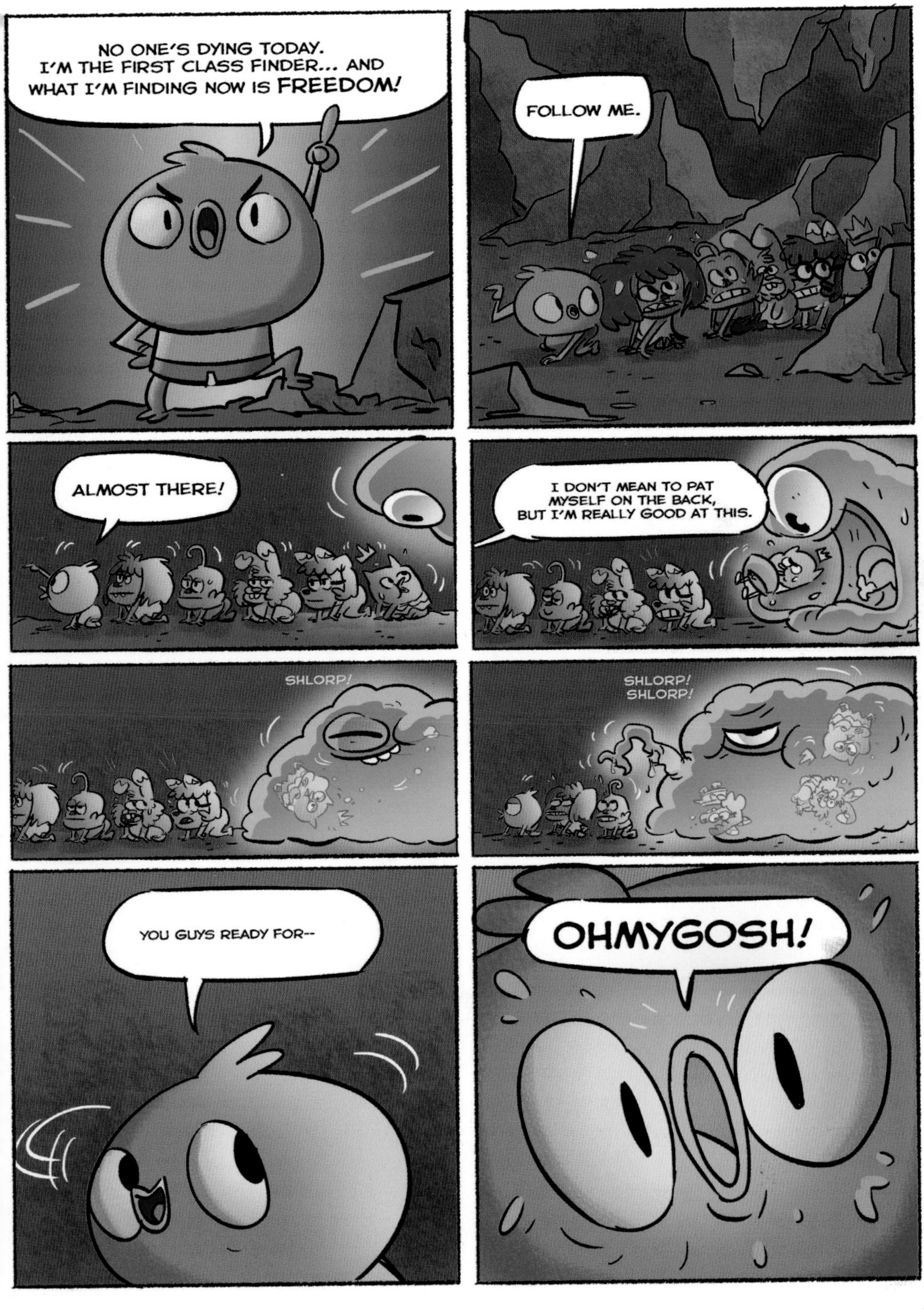
NO ONE'S DYING TODAY. I'M THE FIRST CLASS FINDER... AND WHAT I'M FINDING NOW IS FREEDOM!
FOLLOW ME.
ALMOST THERE!
I DON'T MEAN TO PAT MYSELF ON THE BACK, BUT I'M REALLY GOOD AT THIS.
SHLORP!
SHLORP! SHLORP!
YOU GUYS READY FOR--
OHMYGOSH!

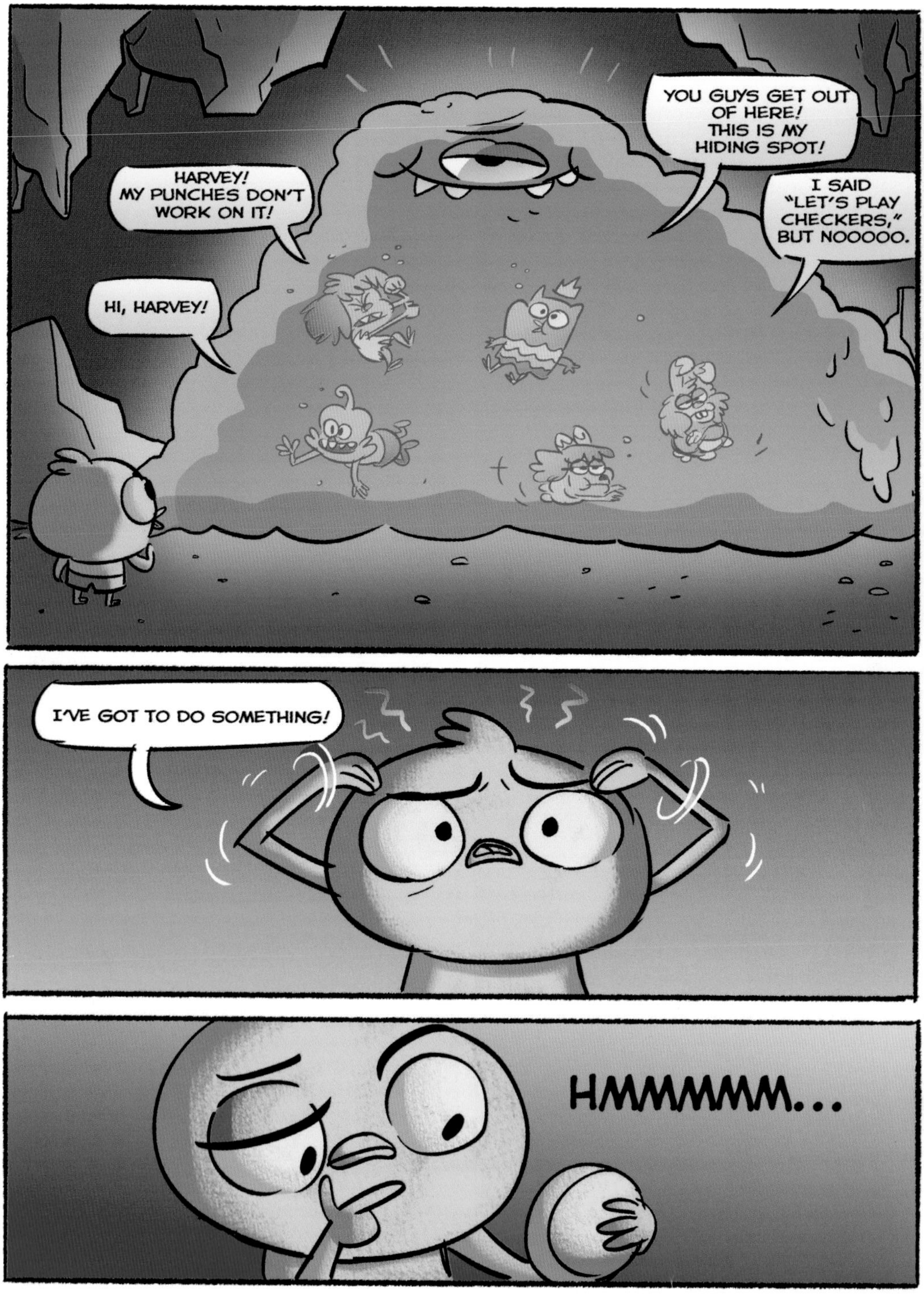
HI, HARVEY!
HARVEY! MY PUNCHES DON'T WORK ON IT!
YOU GUYS GET OUT OF HERE! THIS IS MY HIDING SPOT!
I SAID "LET'S PLAY CHECKERS," BUT NOOOOO.
I'VE GOT TO DO SOMETHING!
HMMMMM...

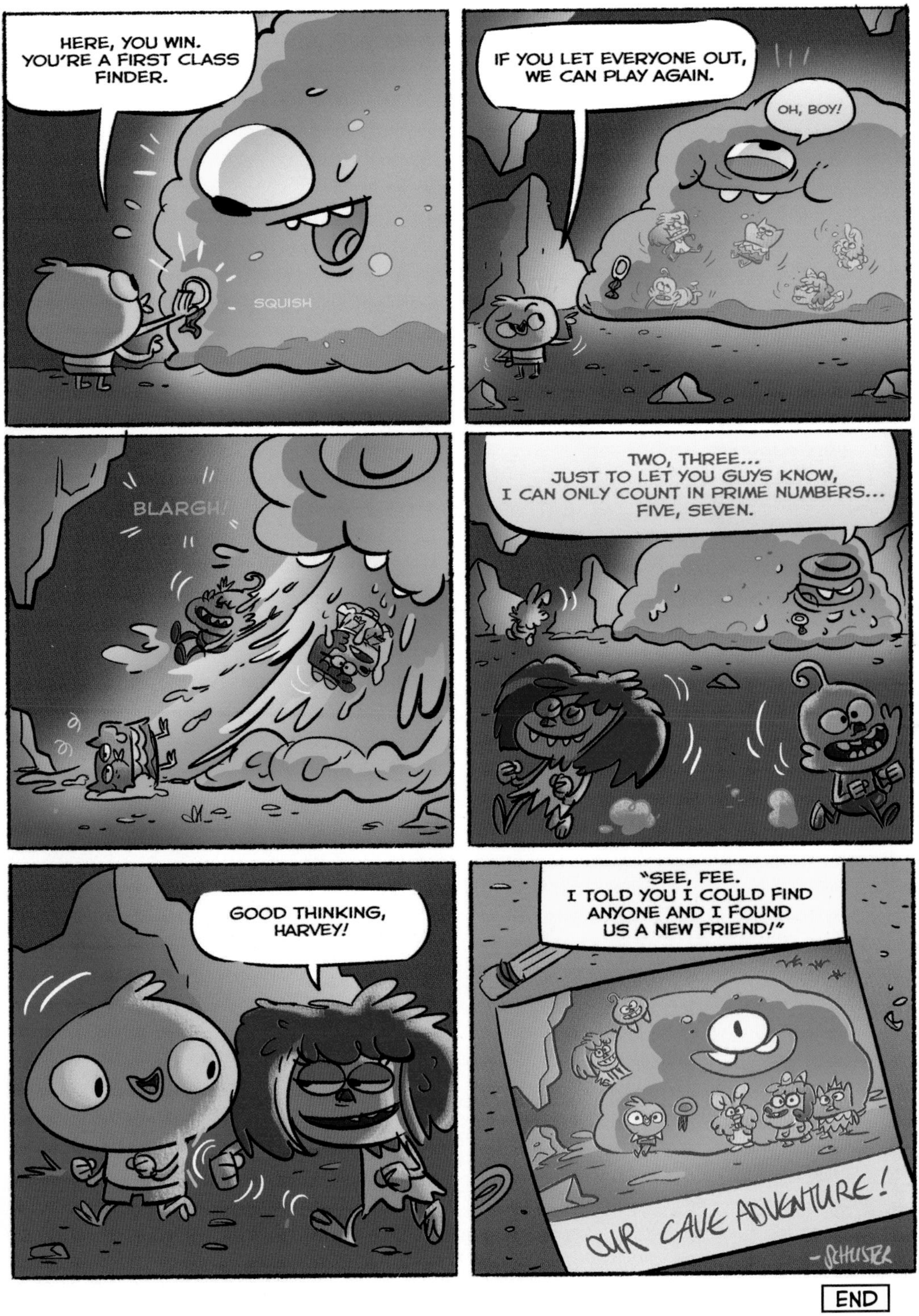
HERE, YOU WIN. YOU'RE A FIRST CLASS FINDER.
SQUISH
IF YOU LET EVERYONE OUT, WE CAN PLAY AGAIN.
OH, BOY!
BLARGH!
TWO, THREE... JUST TO LET YOU GUYS KNOW, I CAN ONLY COUNT IN PRIME NUMBERS... FIVE, SEVEN.
GOOD THINKING, HARVEY!
"SEE, FEE. I TOLD YOU I COULD FIND ANYONE AND I FOUND US A NEW FRIEND!"
OUR CAVE ADVENTURE!
-SCHUSTER
END

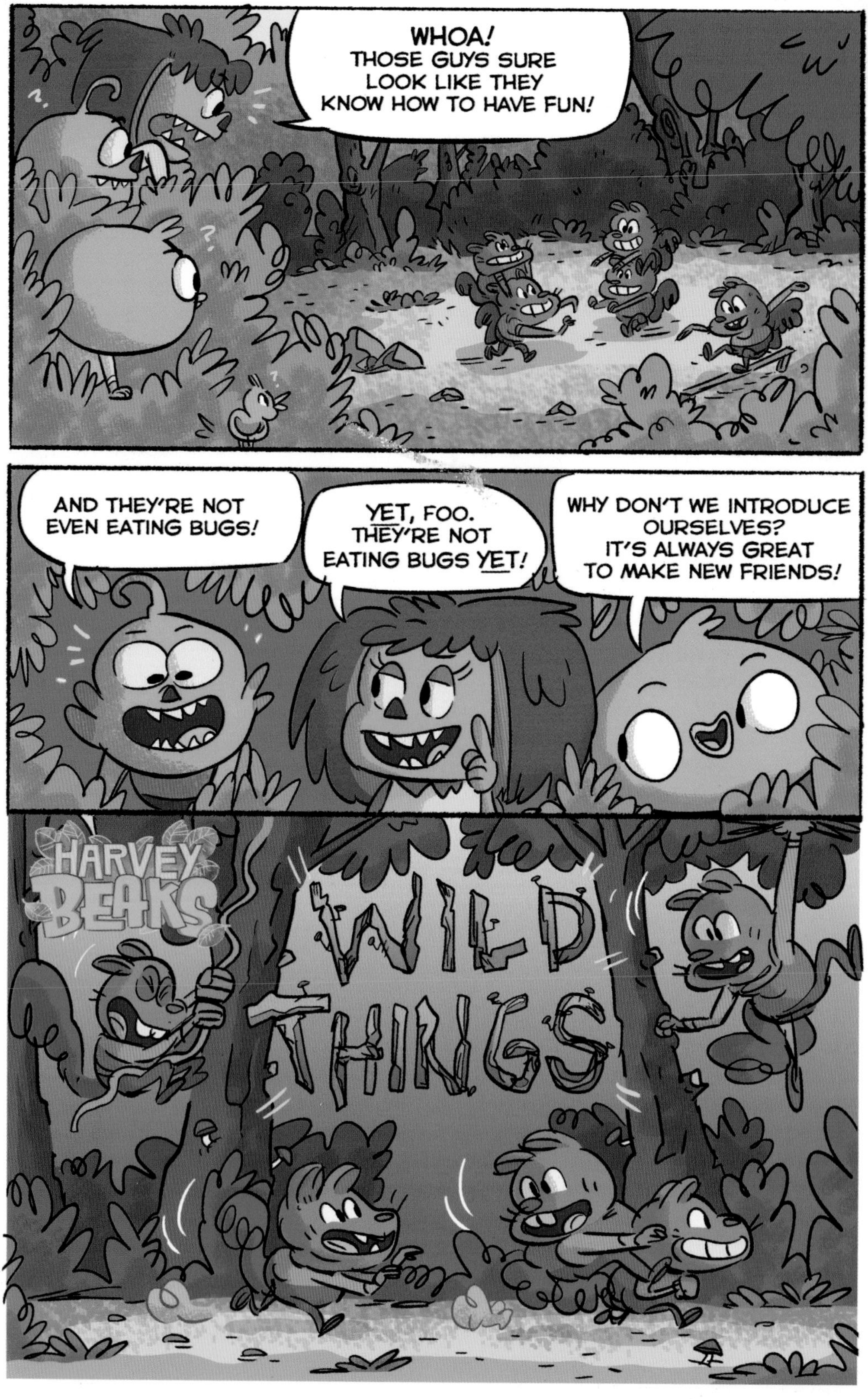
WHOA! THOSE GUYS SURE LOOK LIKE THEY KNOW HOW TO HAVE FUN!
AND THEY'RE NOT EVEN EATING BUGS!
YET, FOO. THEY'RE NOT EATING BUGS YET!
WHY DON'T WE INTRODUCE OURSELVES? IT'S ALWAYS GREAT TO MAKE NEW FRIENDS!
HARVEY BEAKS
WILD THINGS

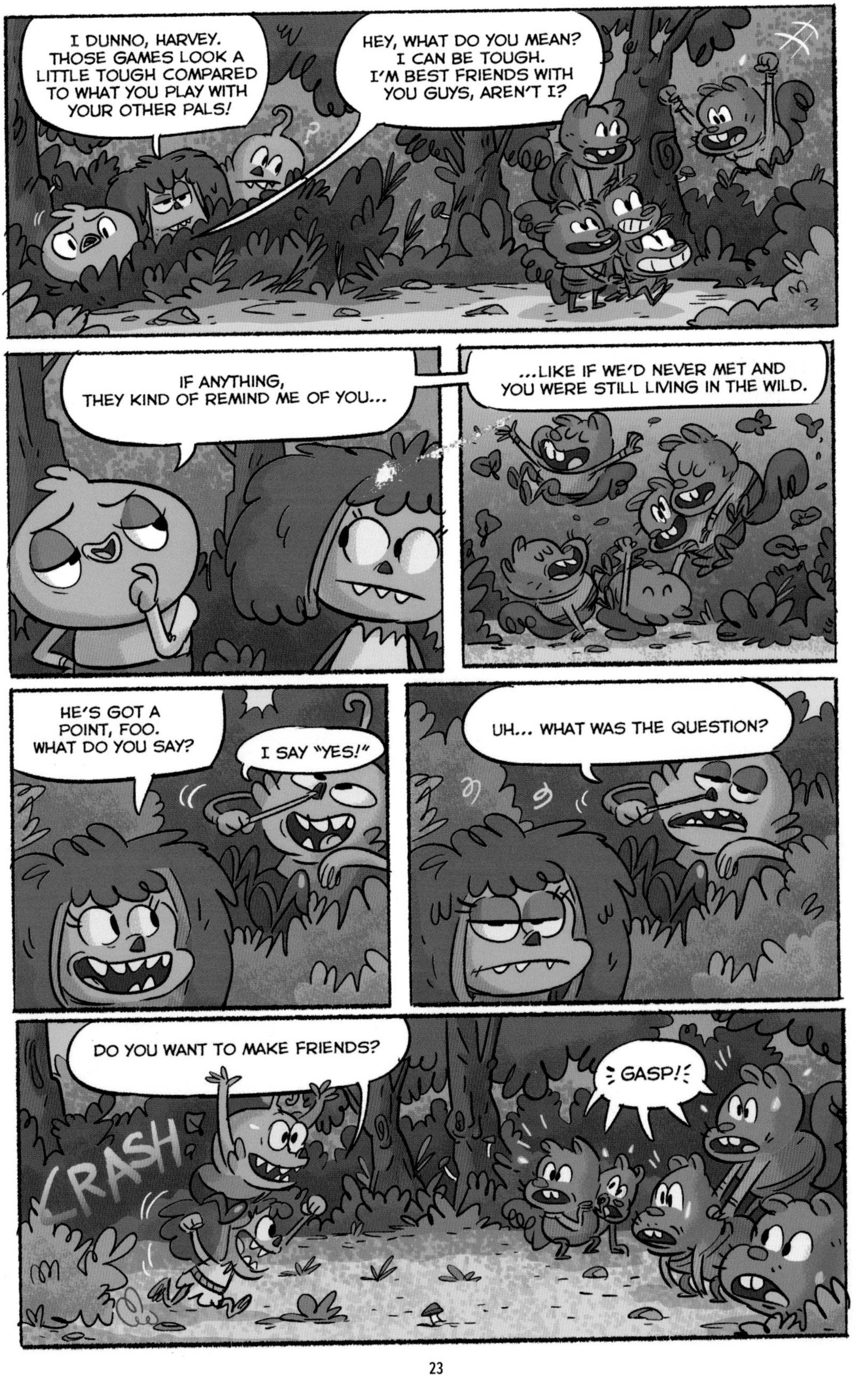
I DUNNO, HARVEY. THOSE GAMES LOOK A LITTLE TOUGH COMPARED TO WHAT YOU PLAY WITH YOUR OTHER PALS!
HEY, WHAT DO YOU MEAN? I CAN BE TOUGH. I'M BEST FRIENDS WITH YOU GUYS, AREN'T I?
IF ANYTHING, THEY KIND OF REMIND ME OF YOU...
...LIKE IF WE'D NEVER MET AND YOU WERE STILL LIVING IN THE WILD.
HE'S GOT A POINT, FOO. WHAT DO YOU SAY?
I SAY "YES!"
UH... WHAT WAS THE QUESTION?
DO YOU WANT TO MAKE FRIENDS?
CRASH
GASP!

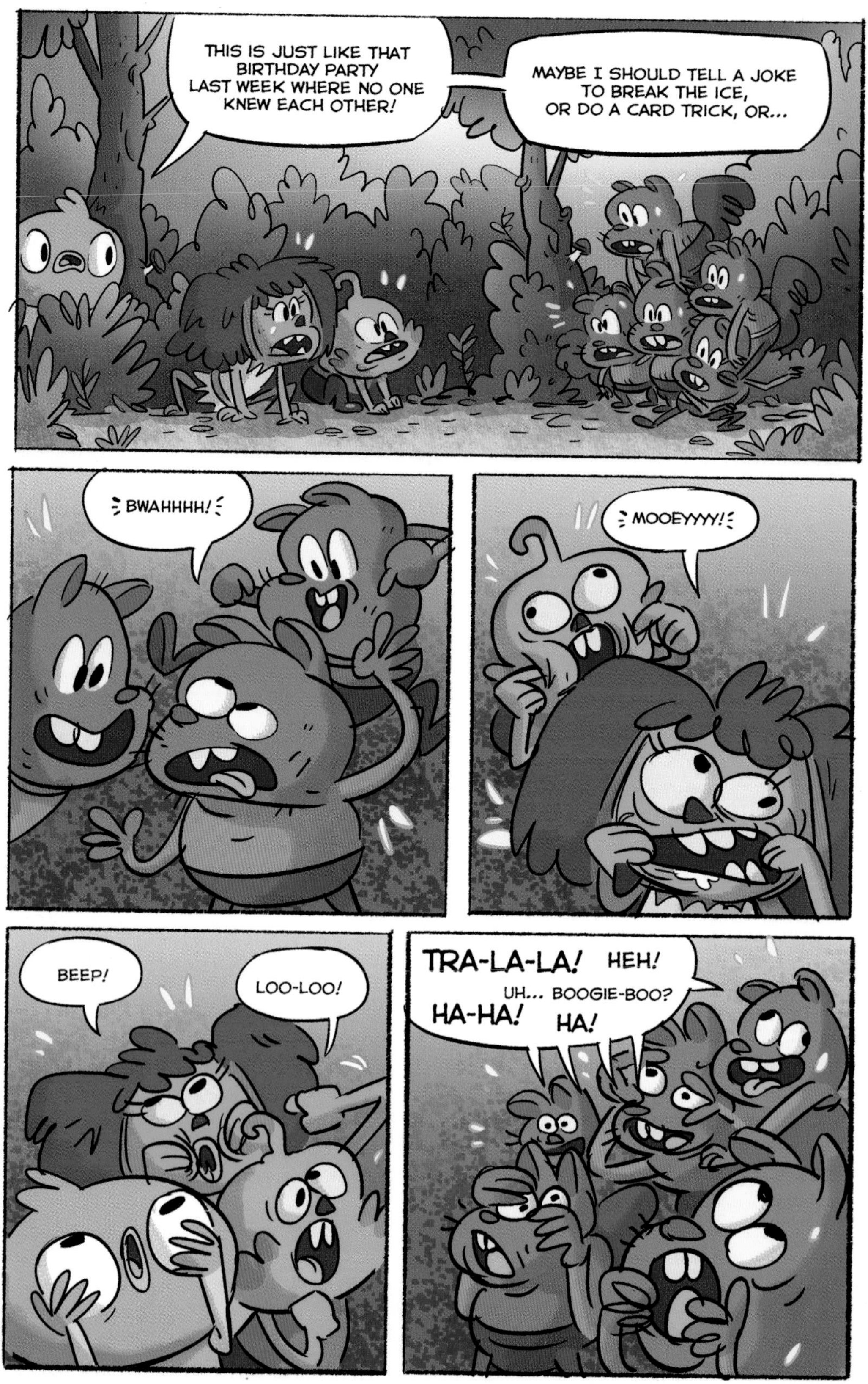
THIS IS JUST LIKE THAT BIRTHDAY PARTY LAST WEEK WHERE NO ONE KNEW EACH OTHER!
MAYBE I SHOULD TELL A JOKE TO BREAK THE ICE, OR DO A CARD TRICK, OR...
BWAHHHH!
MOOEYYYY!
BEEP!
LOO-LOO!
TRA-LA-LA! HEH!
UH... BOOGIE-BOO?
HA-HA! HA!

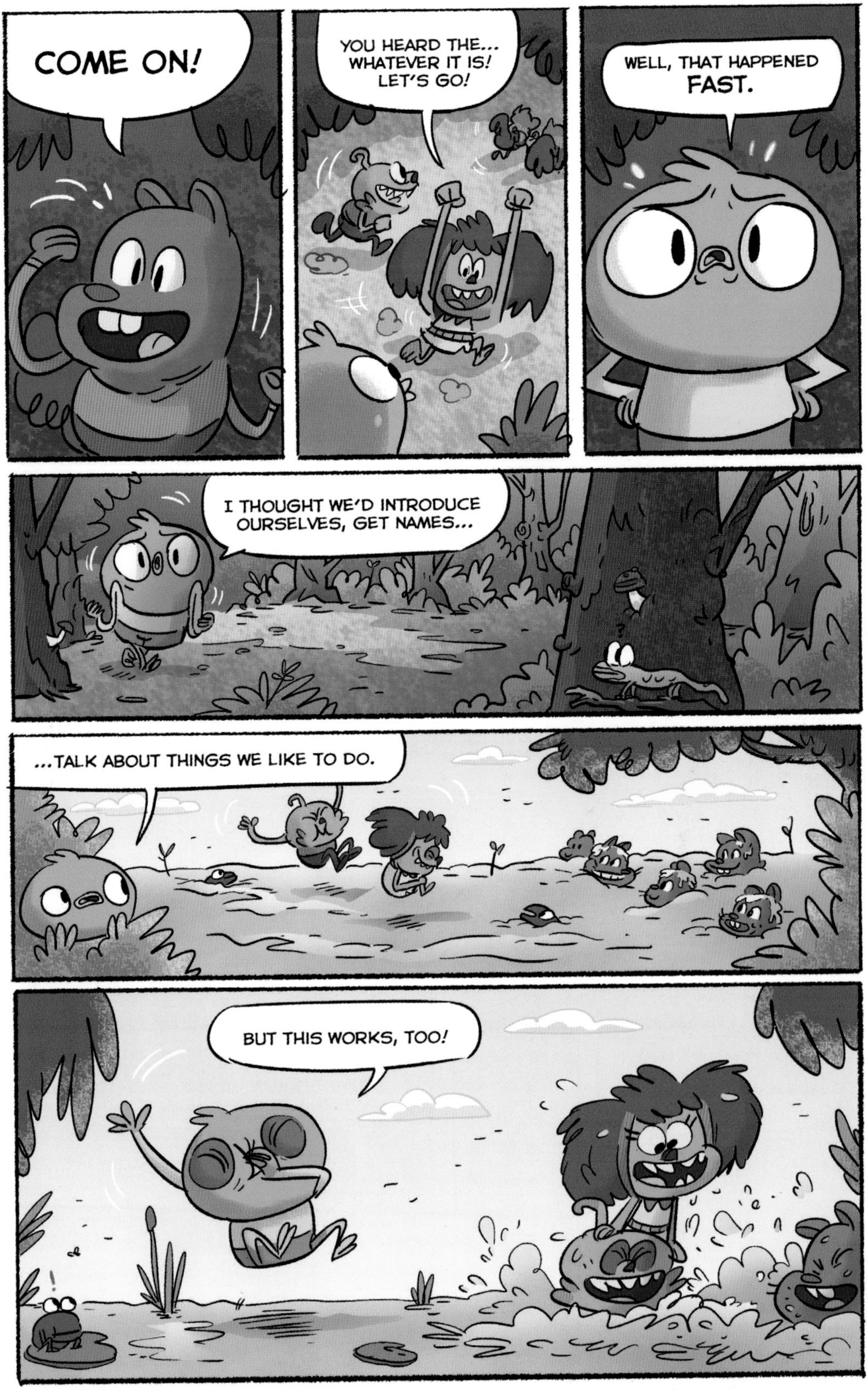
COME ON!
YOU HEARD THE... WHATEVER IT IS! LET'S GO!
WELL, THAT HAPPENED FAST.
I THOUGHT WE'D INTRODUCE OURSELVES, GET NAMES...
...TALK ABOUT THINGS WE LIKE TO DO.
BUT THIS WORKS, TOO!

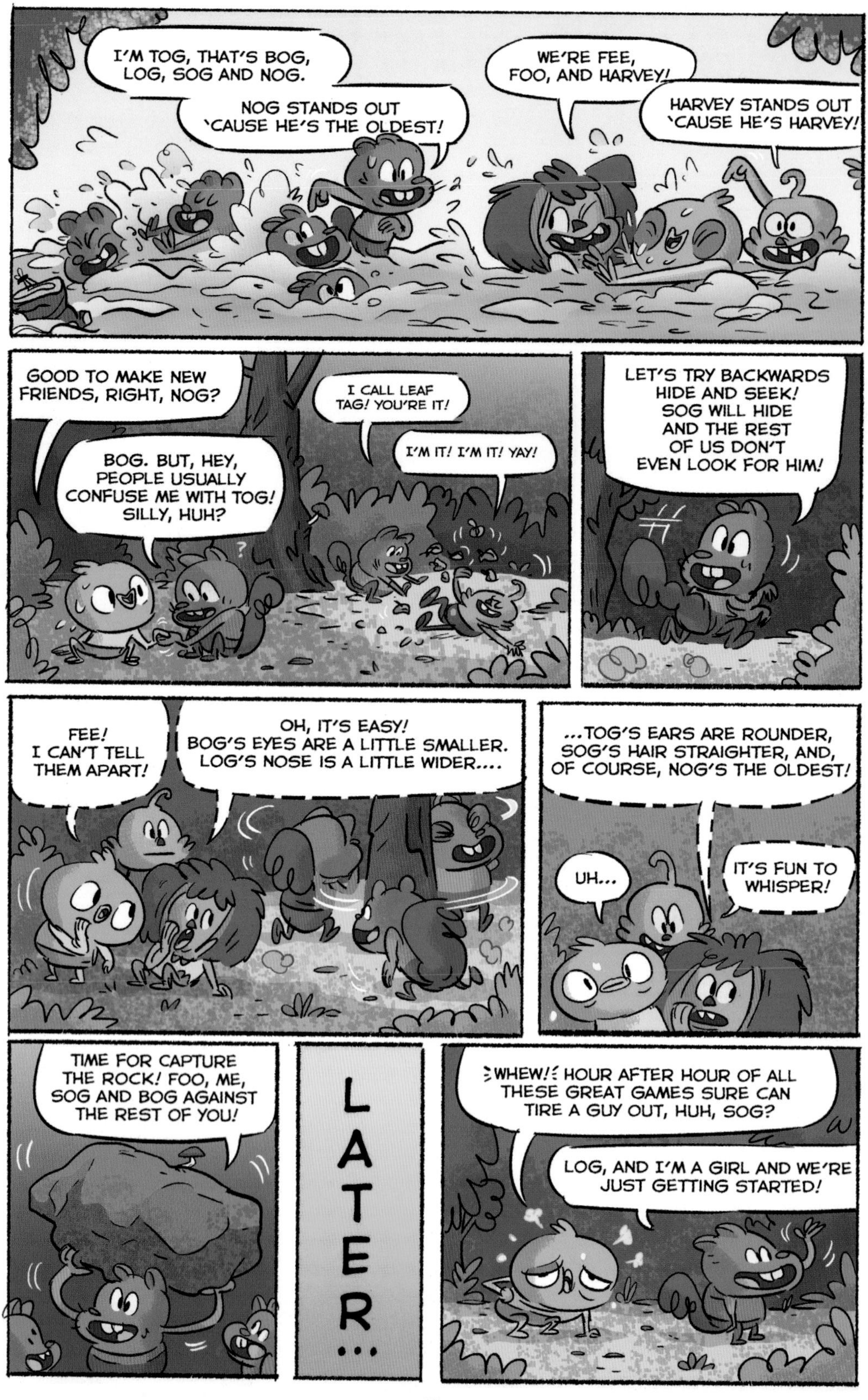

I'M TOG, THAT'S BOG, LOG, SOG AND NOG.
NOG STANDS OUT 'CAUSE HE'S THE OLDEST!
WE'RE FEE, FOO, AND HARVEY!
HARVEY STANDS OUT 'CAUSE HE'S HARVEY!
GOOD TO MAKE NEW FRIENDS, RIGHT, NOG?
BOG. BUT, HEY, PEOPLE USUALLY CONFUSE ME WITH TOG! SILLY, HUH?
I CALL LEAF TAG! YOU'RE IT!
I'M IT! I'M IT! YAY!
LET'S TRY BACKWARDS HIDE AND SEEK! SOG WILL HIDE AND THE REST OF US DON'T EVEN LOOK FOR HIM!
FEE! I CAN'T TELL THEM APART!
OH, IT'S EASY! BOG'S EYES ARE A LITTLE SMALLER. LOG'S NOSE IS A LITTLE WIDER....
...TOG'S EARS ARE ROUNDER, SOG'S HAIR STRAIGHTER, AND, OF COURSE, NOG'S THE OLDEST!
UH...
IT'S FUN TO WHISPER!
TIME FOR CAPTURE THE ROCK! FOO, ME, SOG AND BOG AGAINST THE REST OF YOU!
LATER...
WHEW! HOUR AFTER HOUR OF ALL THESE GREAT GAMES SURE CAN TIRE A GUY OUT, HUH, SOG?
LOG, AND I'M A GIRL AND WE'RE JUST GETTING STARTED!

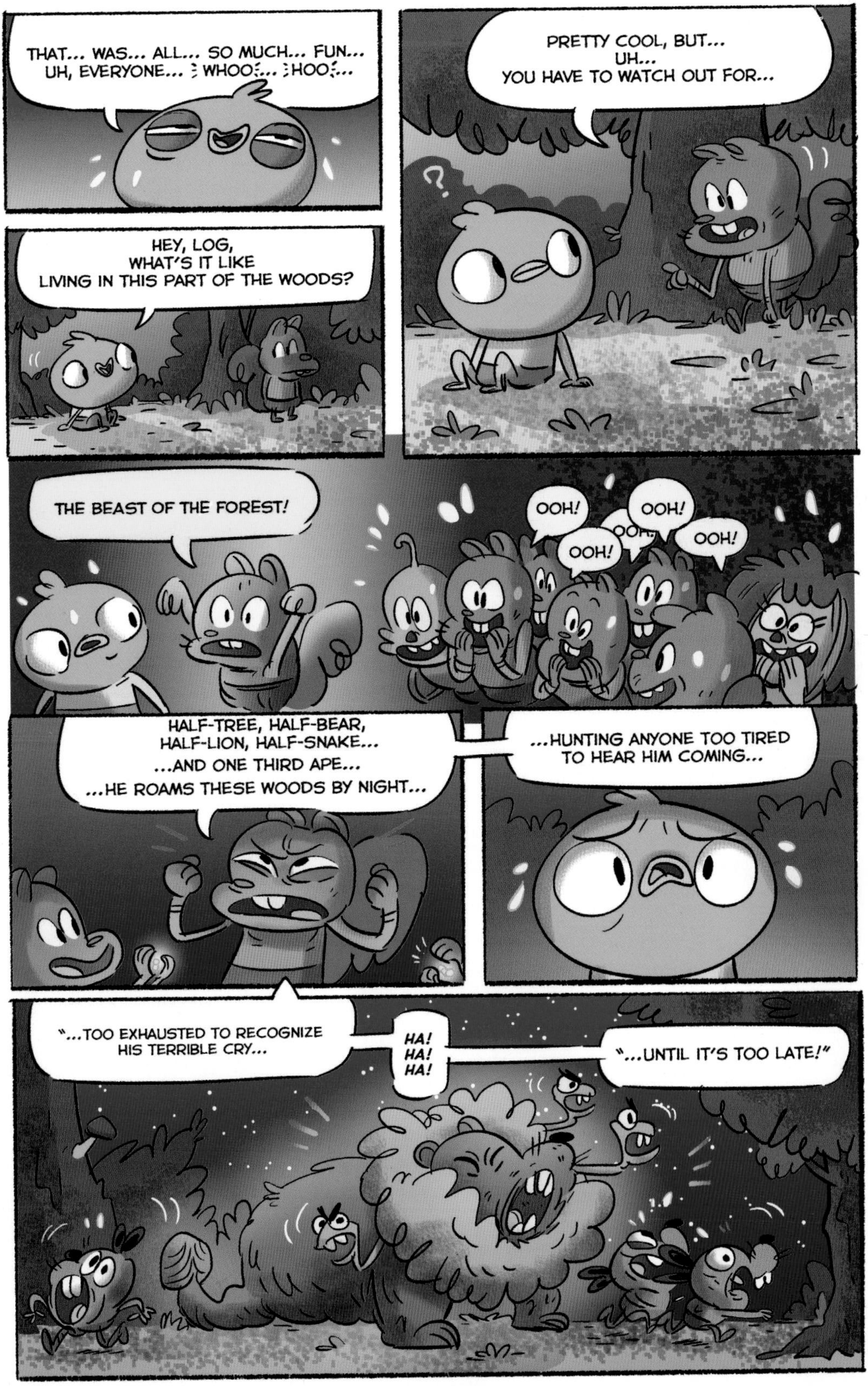
THAT... WAS... ALL... SO MUCH... FUN... UH, EVERYONE... WHOO... HOO...
PRETTY COOL, BUT... UH... YOU HAVE TO WATCH OUT FOR...
HEY, LOG, WHAT'S IT LIKE LIVING IN THIS PART OF THE WOODS?
?
THE BEAST OF THE FOREST!
OOH!
OOH!
OOH!
OOH!
OOH!
HALF-TREE, HALF-BEAR, HALF-LION, HALF-SNAKE... ...AND ONE THIRD APE... ...HE ROAMS THESE WOODS BY NIGHT...
...HUNTING ANYONE TOO TIRED TO HEAR HIM COMING...
"...TOO EXHAUSTED TO RECOGNIZE HIS TERRIBLE CRY...
HA! HA! HA!
"...UNTIL IT'S TOO LATE!"

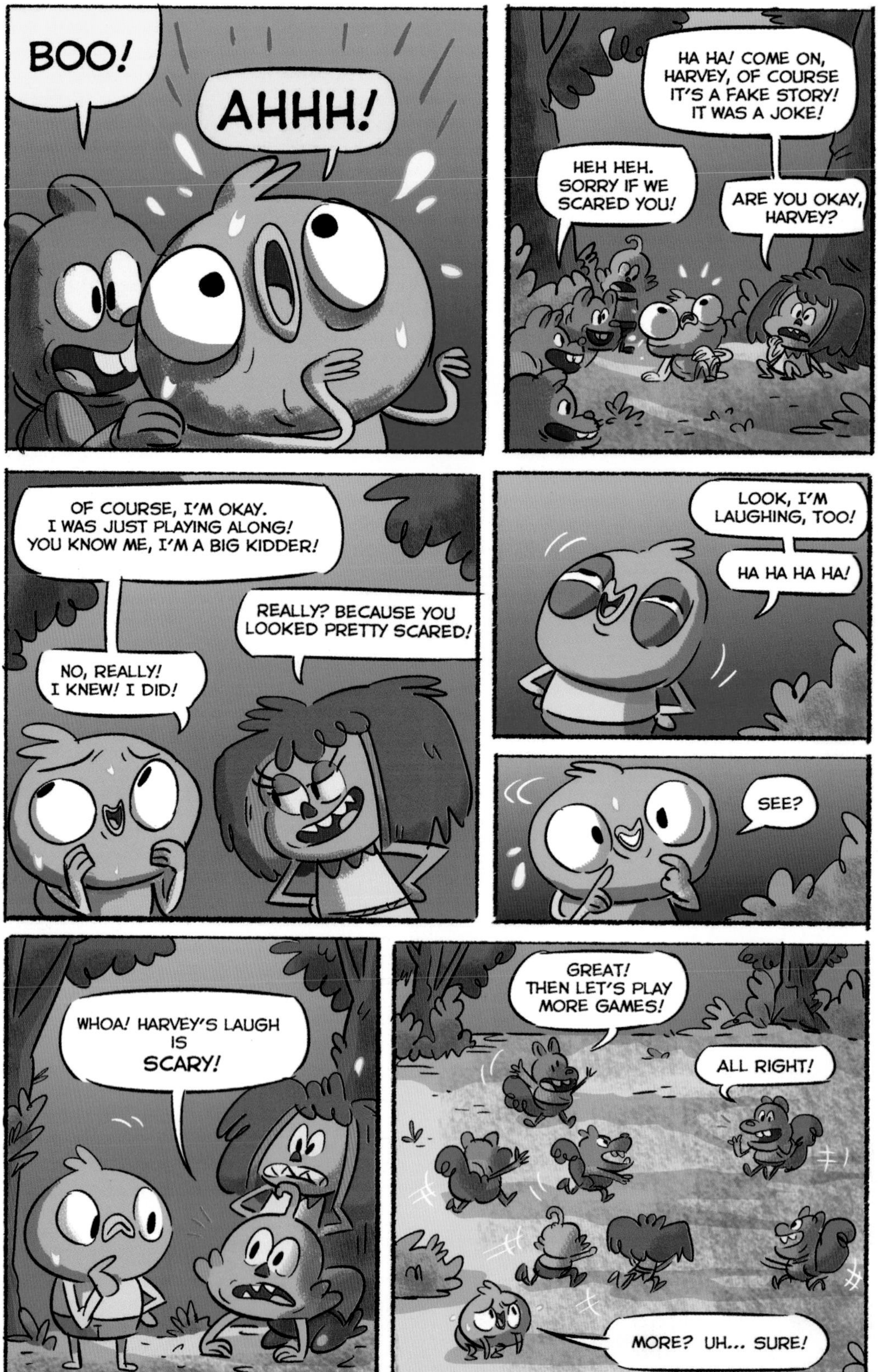
BOO!
AHHH!
HA HA! COME ON, HARVEY, OF COURSE IT'S A FAKE STORY! IT WAS A JOKE!
HEH HEH. SORRY IF WE SCARED YOU!
ARE YOU OKAY, HARVEY?
OF COURSE, I'M OKAY. I WAS JUST PLAYING ALONG! YOU KNOW ME, I'M A BIG KIDDER!
REALLY? BECAUSE YOU LOOKED PRETTY SCARED!
NO, REALLY! I KNEW! I DID!
LOOK, I'M LAUGHING, TOO!
HA HA HA HA!
SEE?
WHOA! HARVEY'S LAUGH IS SCARY!
GREAT! THEN LET'S PLAY MORE GAMES!
ALL RIGHT!
MORE? UH... SURE!

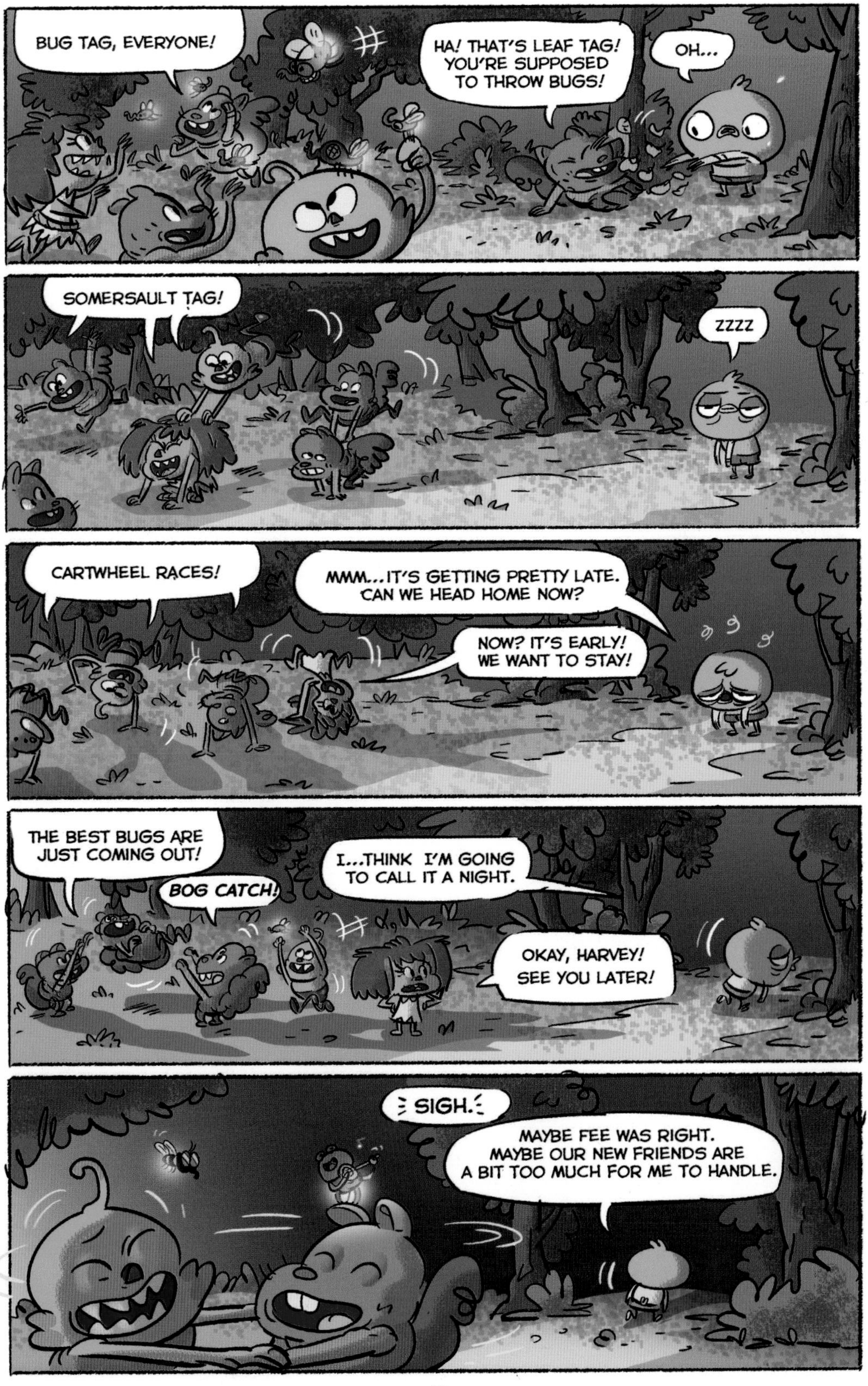
BUG TAG, EVERYONE!
HA! THAT'S LEAF TAG! YOU'RE SUPPOSED TO THROW BUGS!
OH...
SOMERSAULT TAG!
ZZZZ
CARTWHEEL RACES!
MMM...IT'S GETTING PRETTY LATE. CAN WE HEAD HOME NOW?
NOW? IT'S EARLY! WE WANT TO STAY!
THE BEST BUGS ARE JUST COMING OUT!
BOG CATCH!
I...THINK I'M GOING TO CALL IT A NIGHT.
OKAY, HARVEY! SEE YOU LATER!
SIGH.
MAYBE FEE WAS RIGHT. MAYBE OUR NEW FRIENDS ARE A BIT TOO MUCH FOR ME TO HANDLE.

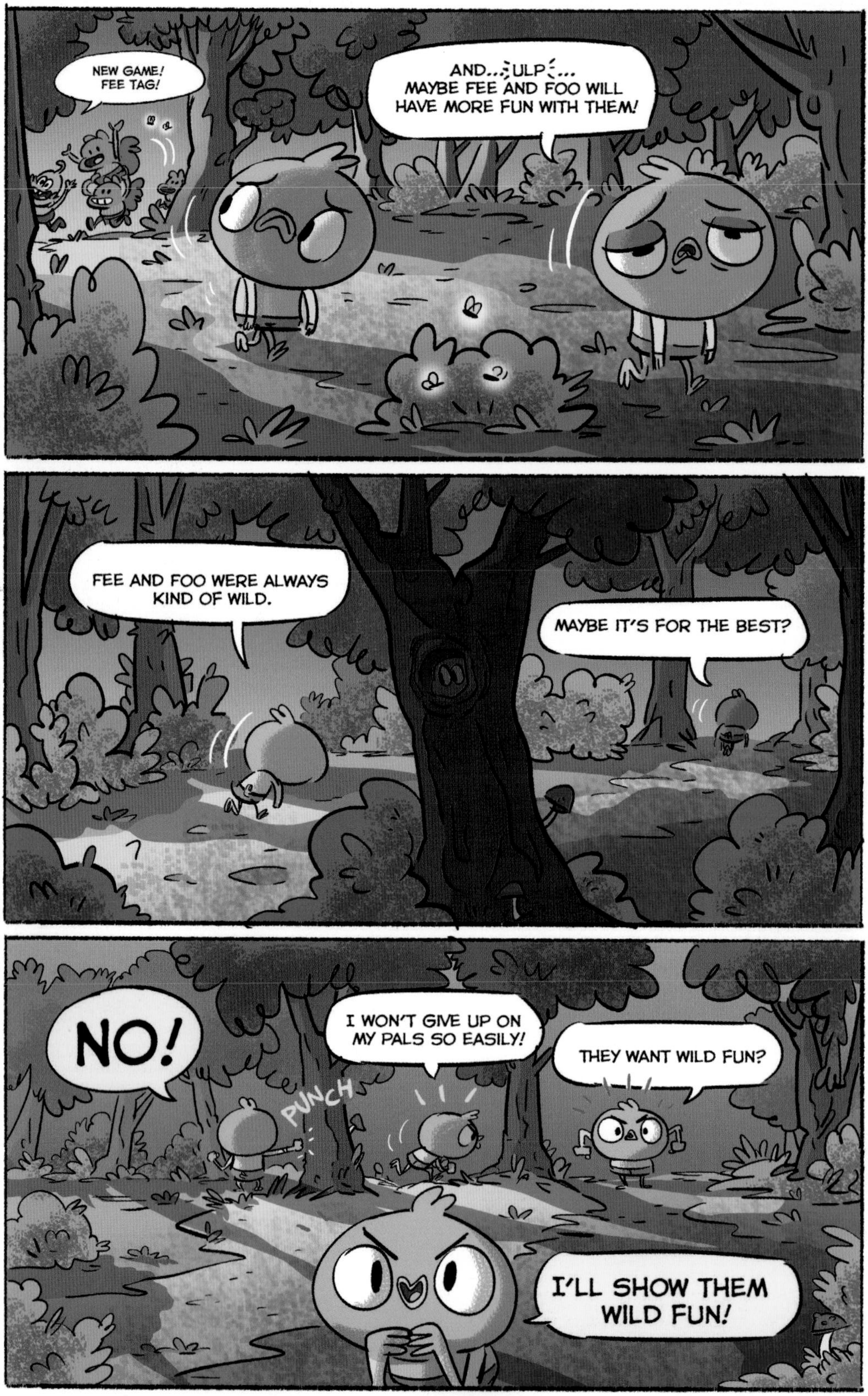
NEW GAME! FEE TAG!
AND... ULP... MAYBE FEE AND FOO WILL HAVE MORE FUN WITH THEM!
FEE AND FOO WERE ALWAYS KIND OF WILD.
MAYBE IT'S FOR THE BEST?
NO!
I WON'T GIVE UP ON MY PALS SO EASILY!
THEY WANT WILD FUN?
PUNCH
I'LL SHOW THEM WILD FUN!

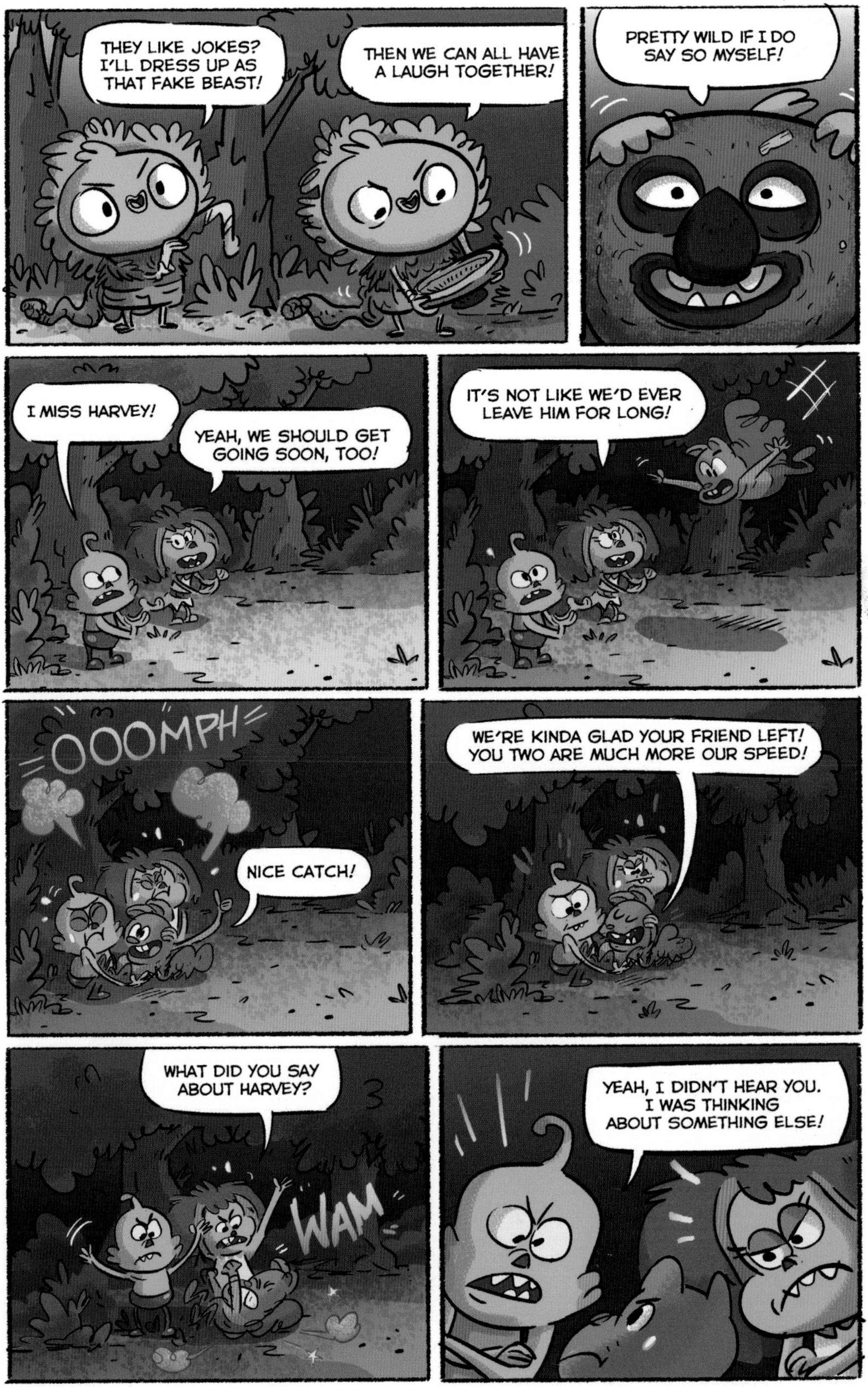
THEY LIKE JOKES? I'LL DRESS UP AS THAT FAKE BEAST!
THEN WE CAN ALL HAVE A LAUGH TOGETHER!
PRETTY WILD IF I DO SAY SO MYSELF!
I MISS HARVEY!
YEAH, WE SHOULD GET GOING SOON, TOO!
IT'S NOT LIKE WE'D EVER LEAVE HIM FOR LONG!
OOOMPH
NICE CATCH!
WE'RE KINDA GLAD YOUR FRIEND LEFT! YOU TWO ARE MUCH MORE OUR SPEED!
WHAT DID YOU SAY ABOUT HARVEY?
WAM
YEAH, I DIDN'T HEAR YOU. I WAS THINKING ABOUT SOMETHING ELSE!

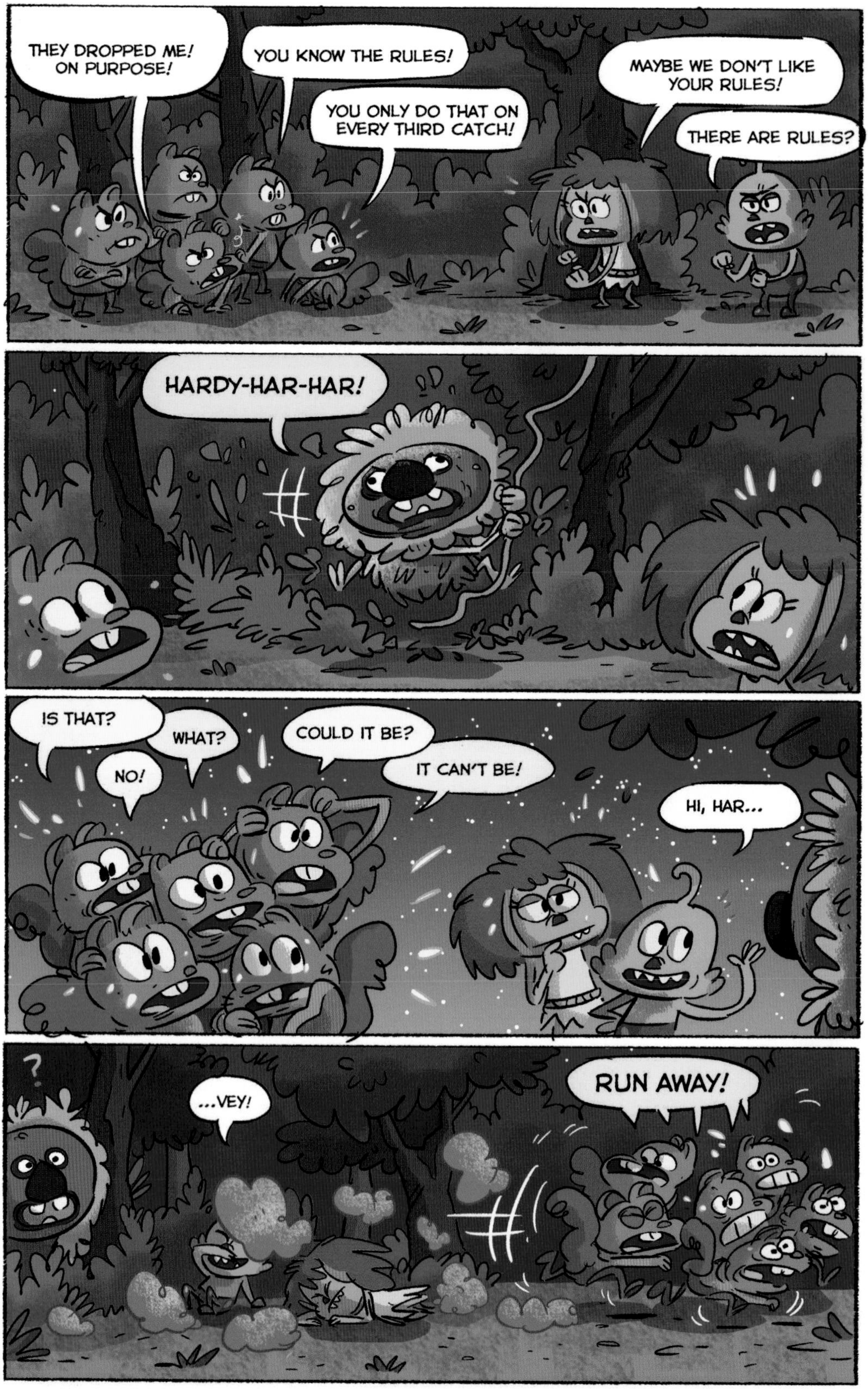
THEY DROPPED ME! ON PURPOSE!
YOU KNOW THE RULES!
YOU ONLY DO THAT ON EVERY THIRD CATCH!
MAYBE WE DON'T LIKE YOUR RULES!
THERE ARE RULES?
HARDY-HAR-HAR!
IS THAT?
WHAT?
NO!
COULD IT BE?
IT CAN'T BE!
HI, HAR...
?
...VEY!
RUN AWAY!

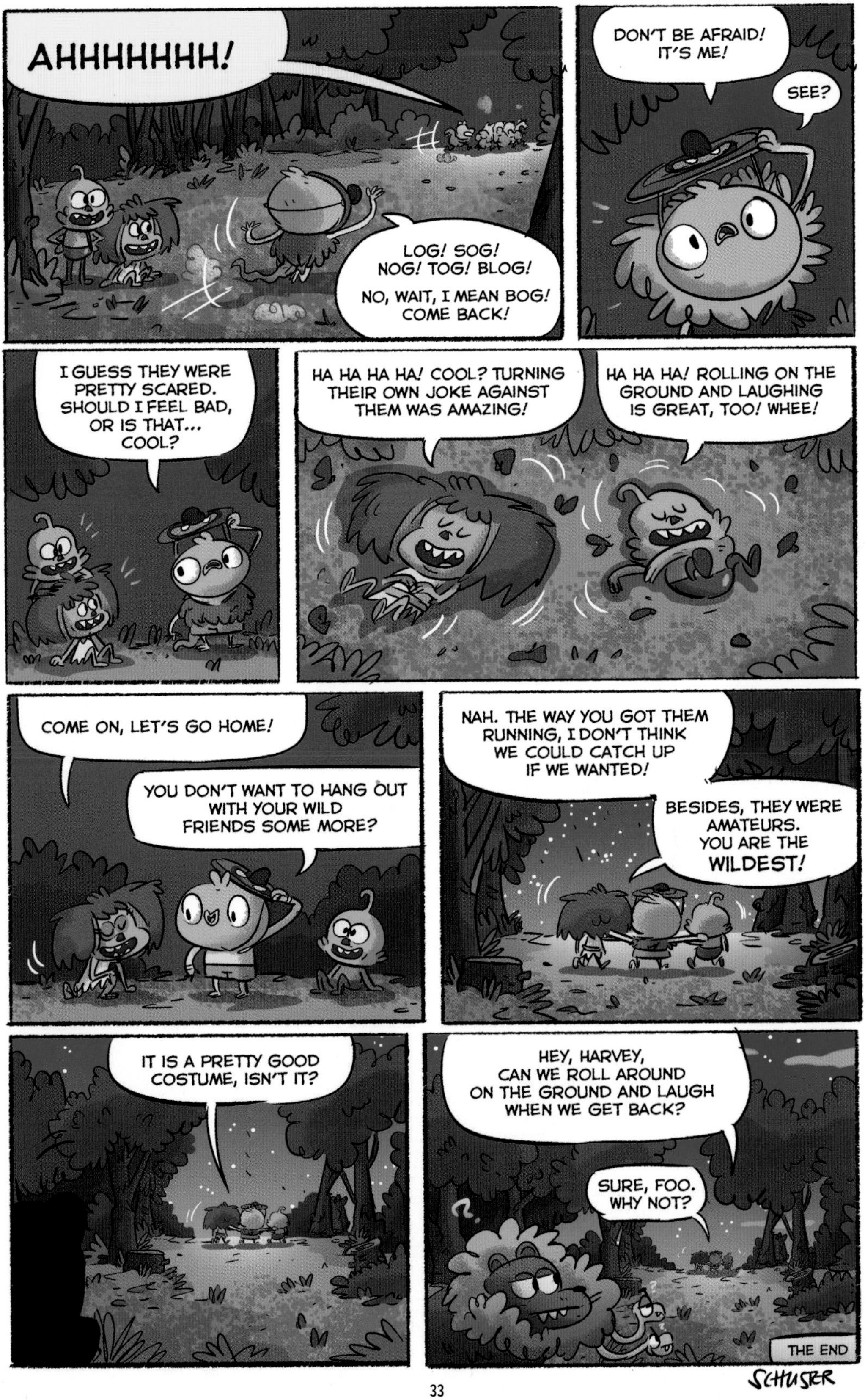
AHHHHHHH!
LOG! SOG! NOG! TOG! BLOG!
NO, WAIT, I MEAN BOG! COME BACK!
DON'T BE AFRAID! IT'S ME!
SEE?
I GUESS THEY WERE PRETTY SCARED. SHOULD I FEEL BAD, OR IS THAT... COOL?
HA HA HA HA! COOL? TURNING THEIR OWN JOKE AGAINST THEM WAS AMAZING!
HA HA HA! ROLLING ON THE GROUND AND LAUGHING IS GREAT, TOO! WHEE!
COME ON, LET'S GO HOME!
YOU DON'T WANT TO HANG OUT WITH YOUR WILD FRIENDS SOME MORE?
NAH. THE WAY YOU GOT THEM RUNNING, I DON'T THINK WE COULD CATCH UP IF WE WANTED!
BESIDES, THEY WERE AMATEURS. YOU ARE THE WILDEST!
IT IS A PRETTY GOOD COSTUME, ISN'T IT?
HEY, HARVEY, CAN WE ROLL AROUND ON THE GROUND AND LAUGH WHEN WE GET BACK?
SURE, FOO. WHY NOT?
THE END
SCHUSTER

HARVEY BEAKS

BUILDIN'

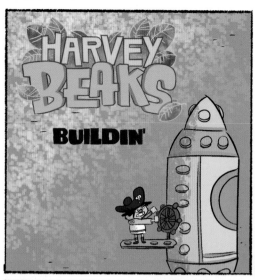

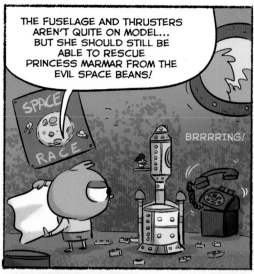

THE FUSELAGE AND THRUSTERS AREN'T QUITE ON MODEL... BUT SHE SHOULD STILL BE ABLE TO RESCUE PRINCESS MARMAR FROM THE EVIL SPACE BEANS!

SPACE RACE

BRRRRING!

THIS IS HARVEY SPEAKING.

'SUP, BRO?

OH, TECHNOBEAR!

'SUP, BRO?

H-MAN, LEMME CUT TO DA CHASE.

MAX BRUTEIN

YOU SEEM LIKE A MAN OF MANY TALENTS. YOU KNOW ANYTHING ABOUT BUILDIN'?

FIRST OFF, WOW. THAT'S REALLY FLATTERING, DUDE. SECONDLY, YEAH! HECK, I'M BUILDIN' AS WE SPEAK!

SWEET! SEE, THERE'S A JUNIOR BUILDIN' COMPETITION TODAY AT THE REC CENTER. BUT IT'S A TEAM THING AND I DON'T HAVE A PARTNER.

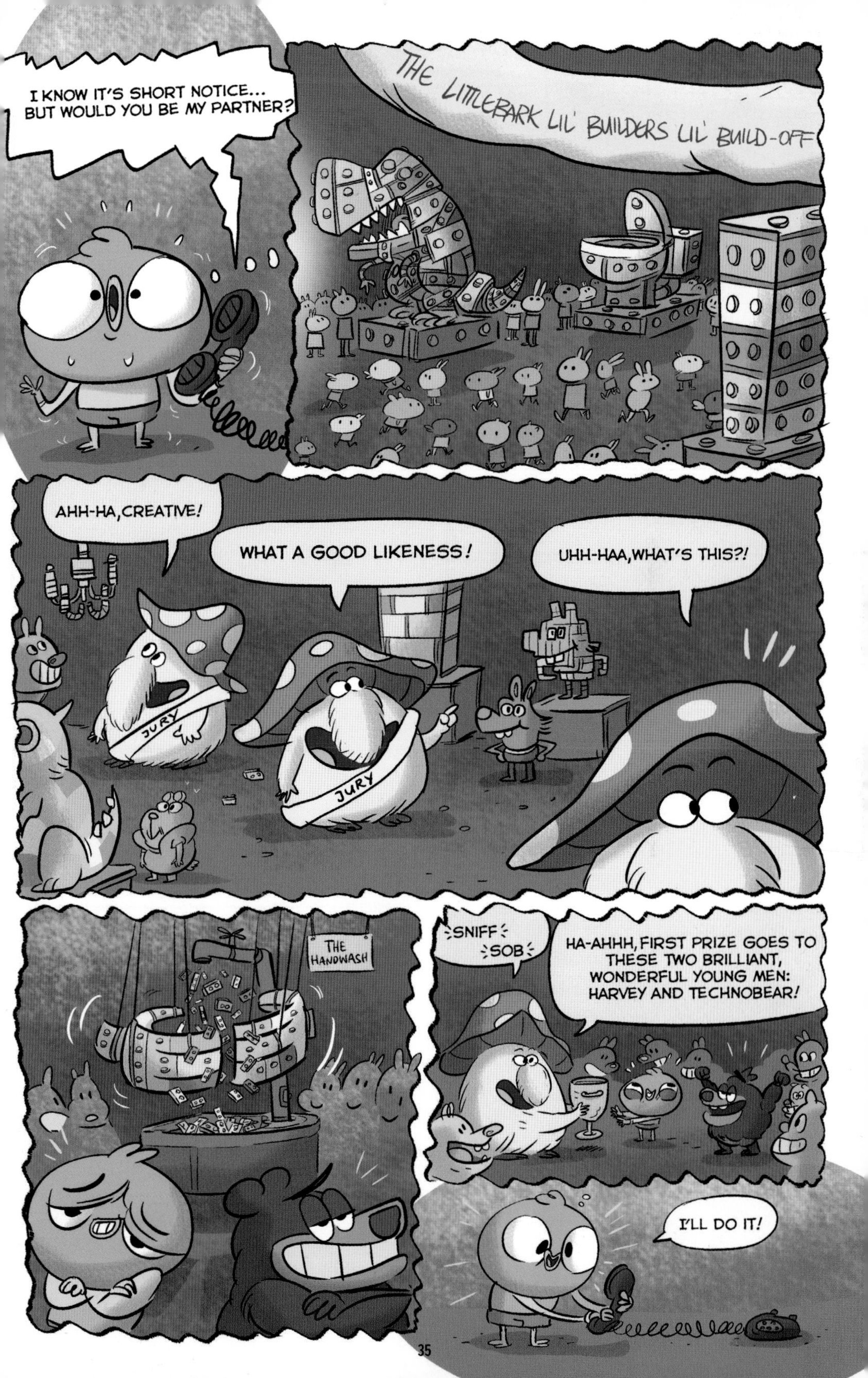
I KNOW IT'S SHORT NOTICE... BUT WOULD YOU BE MY PARTNER?
THE LITTLEBARK LIL' BUILDERS LIL' BUILD-OFF
AHH-HA, CREATIVE!
WHAT A GOOD LIKENESS!
UHH-HAA, WHAT'S THIS?!
JURY
JURY
THE HANDWASH
SNIFF
SOB
HA-AHHH, FIRST PRIZE GOES TO THESE TWO BRILLIANT, WONDERFUL YOUNG MEN: HARVEY AND TECHNOBEAR!
I'LL DO IT!

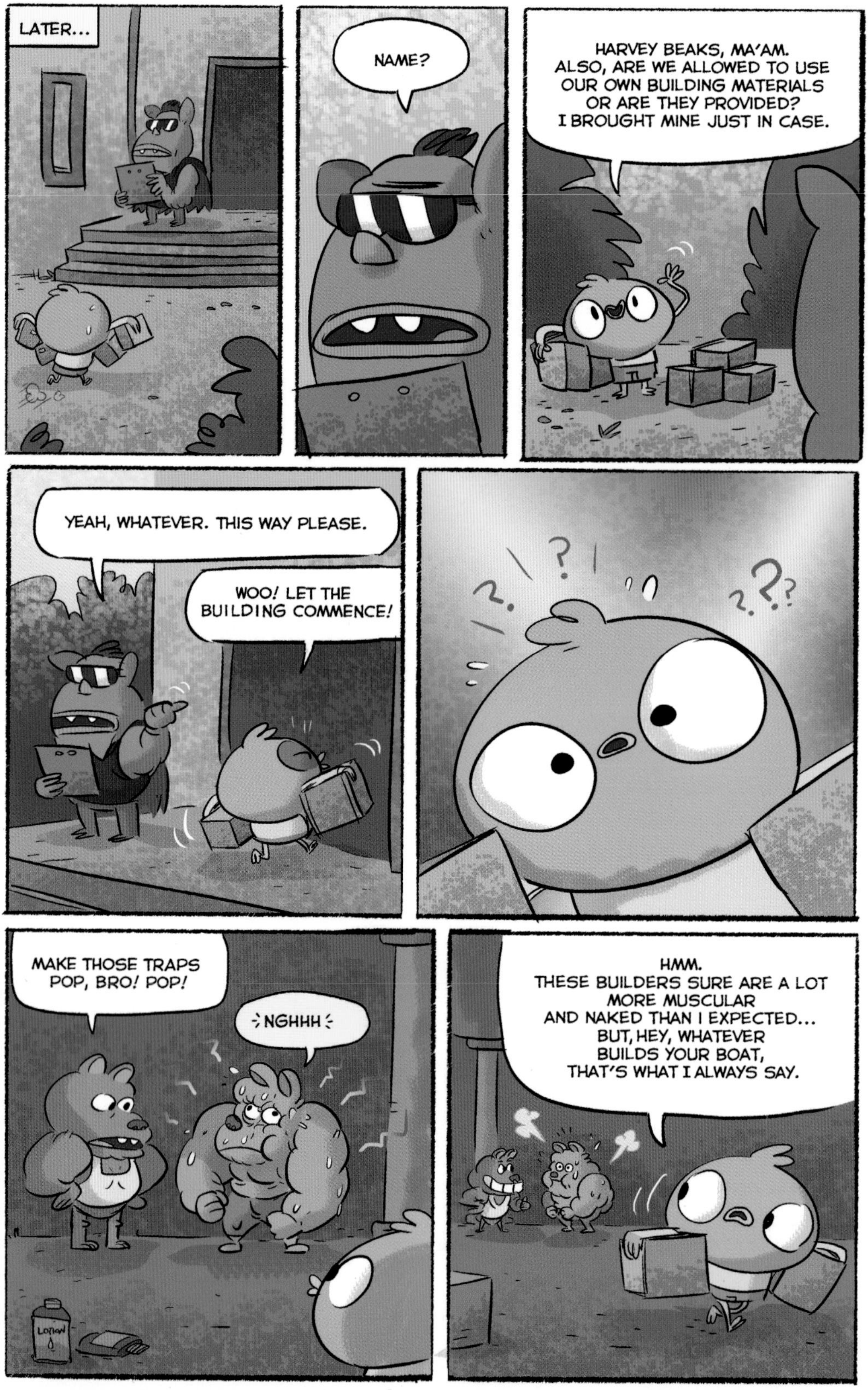
LATER...
NAME?
HARVEY BEAKS, MA'AM. ALSO, ARE WE ALLOWED TO USE OUR OWN BUILDING MATERIALS OR ARE THEY PROVIDED? I BROUGHT MINE JUST IN CASE.
YEAH, WHATEVER. THIS WAY PLEASE.
WOO! LET THE BUILDING COMMENCE!
MAKE THOSE TRAPS POP, BRO! POP!
NGHHH
LOTION
HMM. THESE BUILDERS SURE ARE A LOT MORE MUSCULAR AND NAKED THAN I EXPECTED... BUT, HEY, WHATEVER BUILDS YOUR BOAT, THAT'S WHAT I ALWAYS SAY.

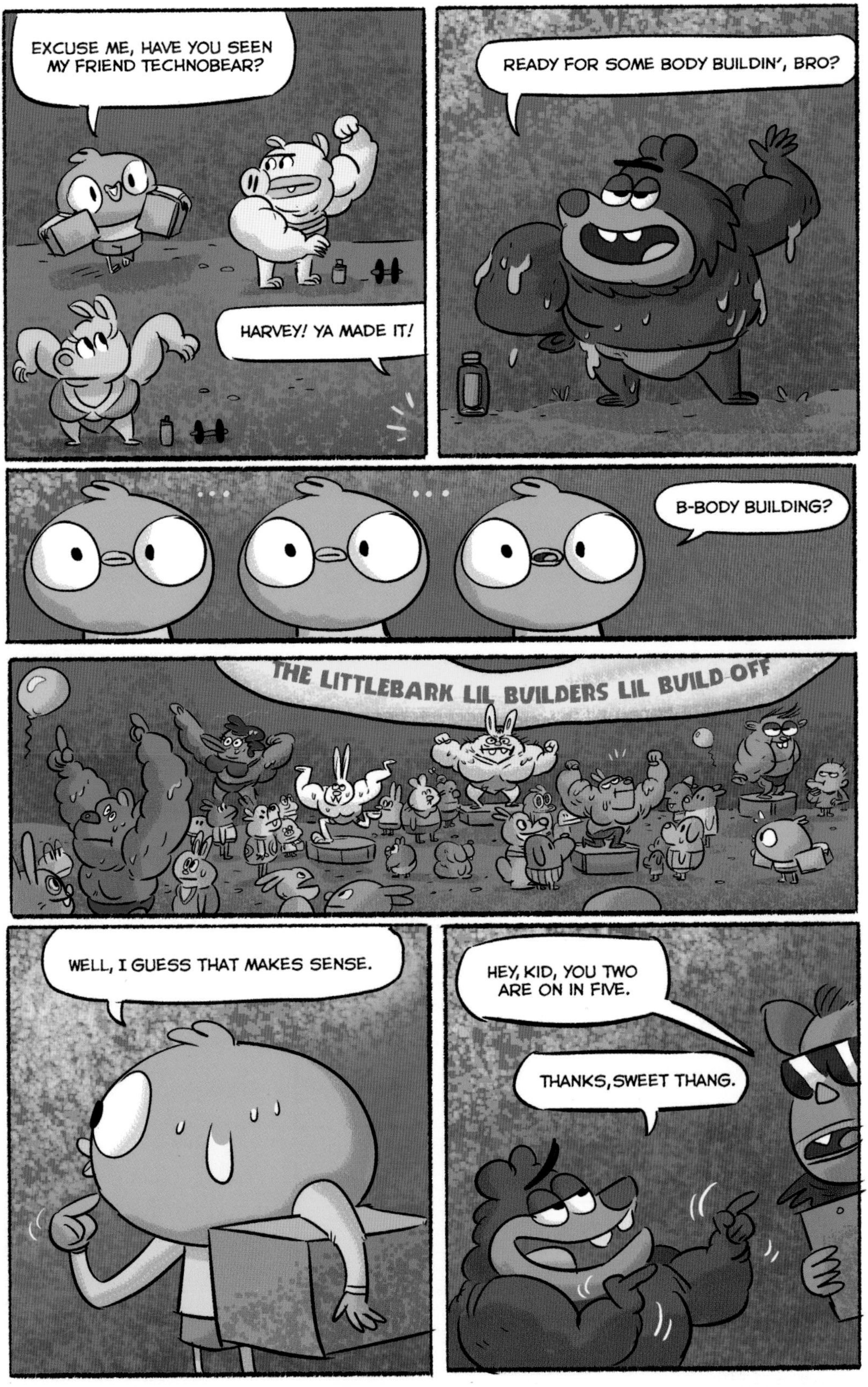
EXCUSE ME, HAVE YOU SEEN MY FRIEND TECHNOBEAR?
HARVEY! YA MADE IT!
READY FOR SOME BODY BUILDIN', BRO?
...
...
B-BODY BUILDING?
THE LITTLEBARK LIL BUILDERS LIL BUILD-OFF
WELL, I GUESS THAT MAKES SENSE.
HEY, KID, YOU TWO ARE ON IN FIVE.
THANKS, SWEET THANG.

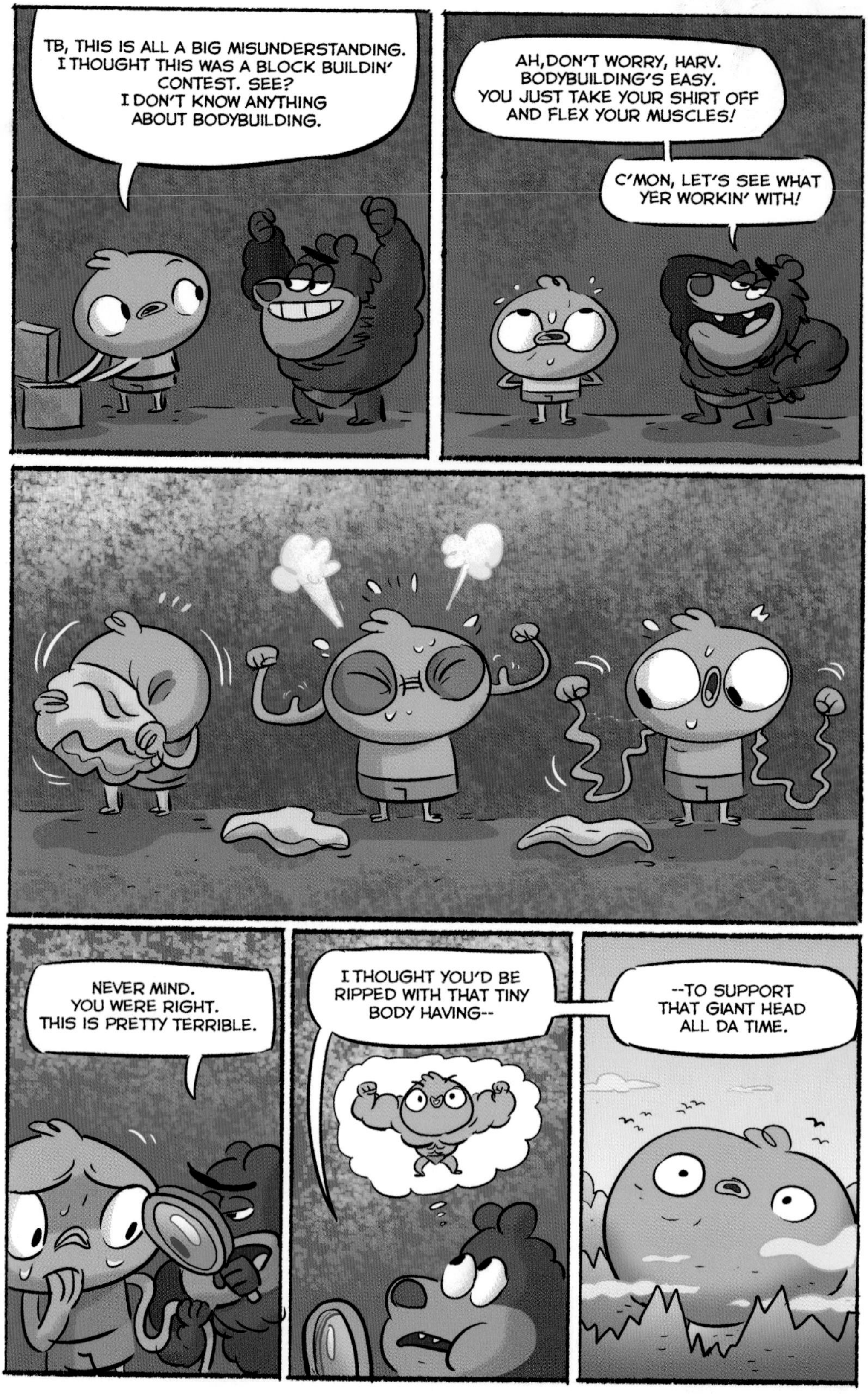
TB, THIS IS ALL A BIG MISUNDERSTANDING. I THOUGHT THIS WAS A BLOCK BUILDIN' CONTEST. SEE? I DON'T KNOW ANYTHING ABOUT BODYBUILDING.
AH, DON'T WORRY, HARV. BODYBUILDING'S EASY. YOU JUST TAKE YOUR SHIRT OFF AND FLEX YOUR MUSCLES!
C'MON, LET'S SEE WHAT YER WORKIN' WITH!
NEVER MIND. YOU WERE RIGHT. THIS IS PRETTY TERRIBLE.
I THOUGHT YOU'D BE RIPPED WITH THAT TINY BODY HAVING--
--TO SUPPORT THAT GIANT HEAD ALL DA TIME.

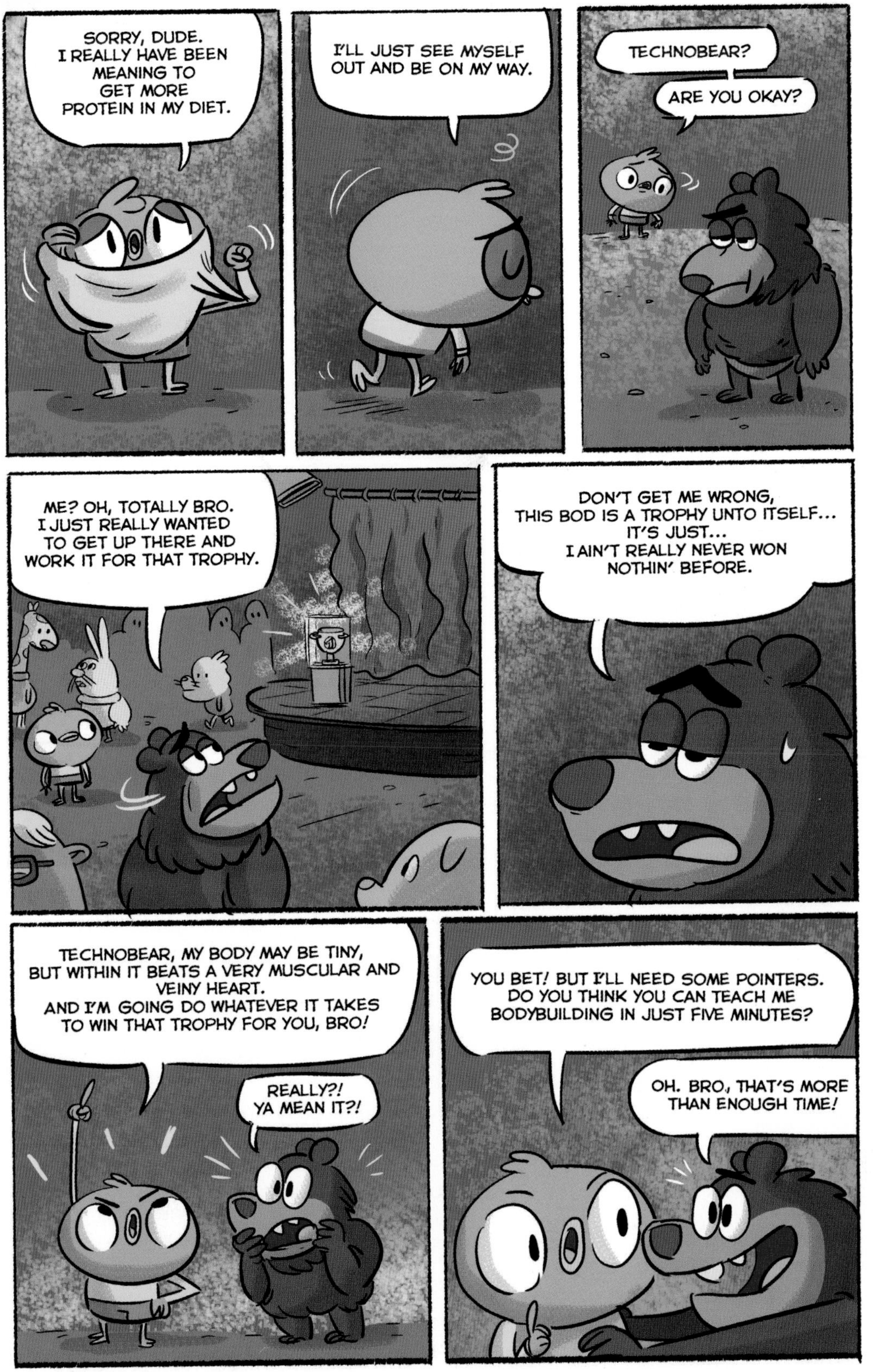
SORRY, DUDE. I REALLY HAVE BEEN MEANING TO GET MORE PROTEIN IN MY DIET.
I'LL JUST SEE MYSELF OUT AND BE ON MY WAY.
TECHNOBEAR?
ARE YOU OKAY?
ME? OH, TOTALLY BRO. I JUST REALLY WANTED TO GET UP THERE AND WORK IT FOR THAT TROPHY.
DON'T GET ME WRONG, THIS BOD IS A TROPHY UNTO ITSELF... IT'S JUST... I AIN'T REALLY NEVER WON NOTHIN' BEFORE.
TECHNOBEAR, MY BODY MAY BE TINY, BUT WITHIN IT BEATS A VERY MUSCULAR AND VEINY HEART. AND I'M GOING DO WHATEVER IT TAKES TO WIN THAT TROPHY FOR YOU, BRO!
REALLY?! YA MEAN IT?!
YOU BET! BUT I'LL NEED SOME POINTERS. DO YOU THINK YOU CAN TEACH ME BODYBUILDING IN JUST FIVE MINUTES?
OH. BRO, THAT'S MORE THAN ENOUGH TIME!

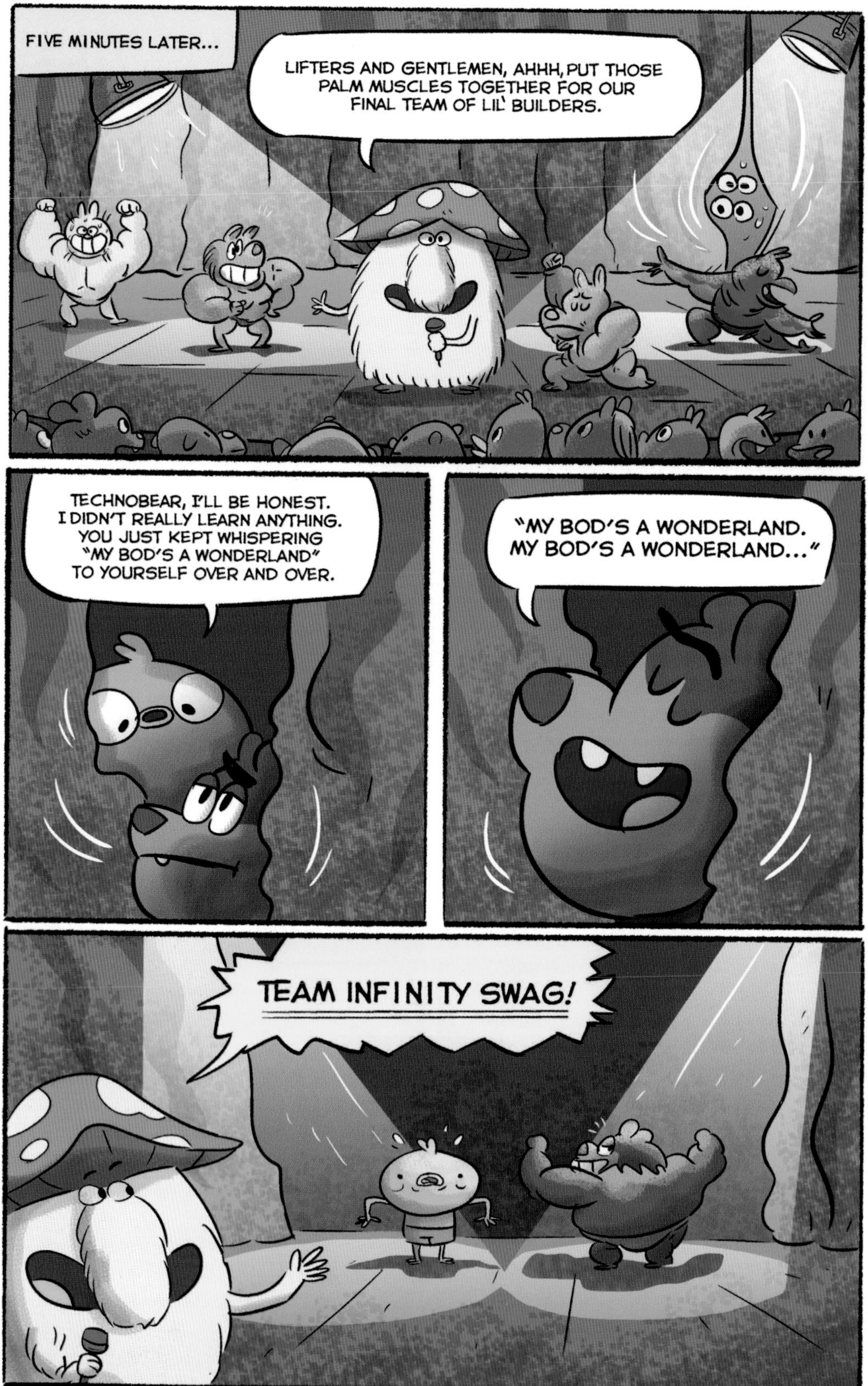
FIVE MINUTES LATER...
LIFTERS AND GENTLEMEN, AHHH, PUT THOSE PALM MUSCLES TOGETHER FOR OUR FINAL TEAM OF LIL' BUILDERS.
TECHNOBEAR, I'LL BE HONEST. I DIDN'T REALLY LEARN ANYTHING. YOU JUST KEPT WHISPERING "MY BOD'S A WONDERLAND" TO YOURSELF OVER AND OVER.
"MY BOD'S A WONDERLAND. MY BOD'S A WONDERLAND..."
TEAM INFINITY SWAG!

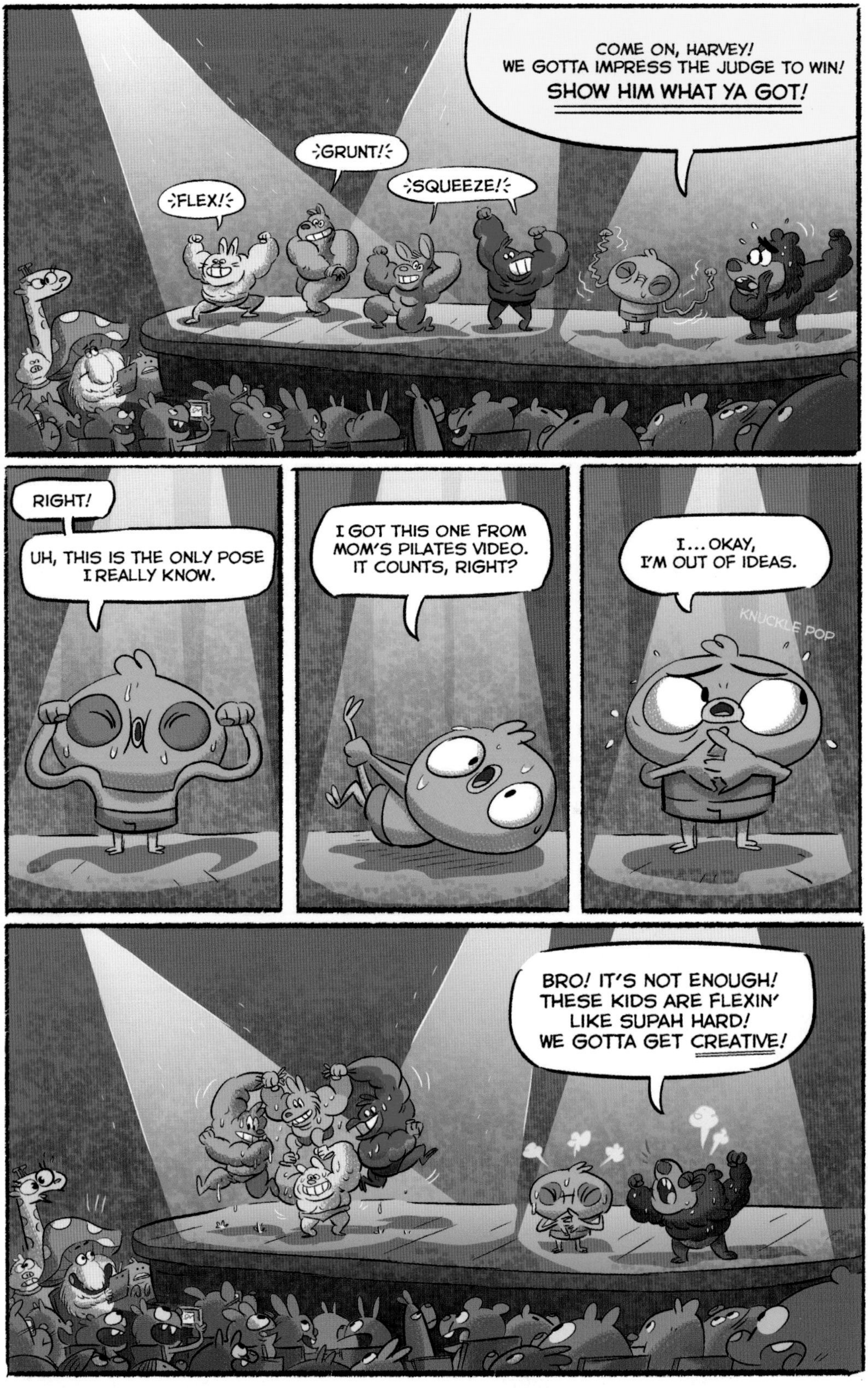
COME ON, HARVEY! WE GOTTA IMPRESS THE JUDGE TO WIN! SHOW HIM WHAT YA GOT!
FLEX!
GRUNT!
SQUEEZE!
RIGHT!
UH, THIS IS THE ONLY POSE I REALLY KNOW.
I GOT THIS ONE FROM MOM'S PILATES VIDEO. IT COUNTS, RIGHT?
I...OKAY, I'M OUT OF IDEAS.
KNUCKLE POP
BRO! IT'S NOT ENOUGH! THESE KIDS ARE FLEXIN' LIKE SUPAH HARD! WE GOTTA GET CREATIVE!

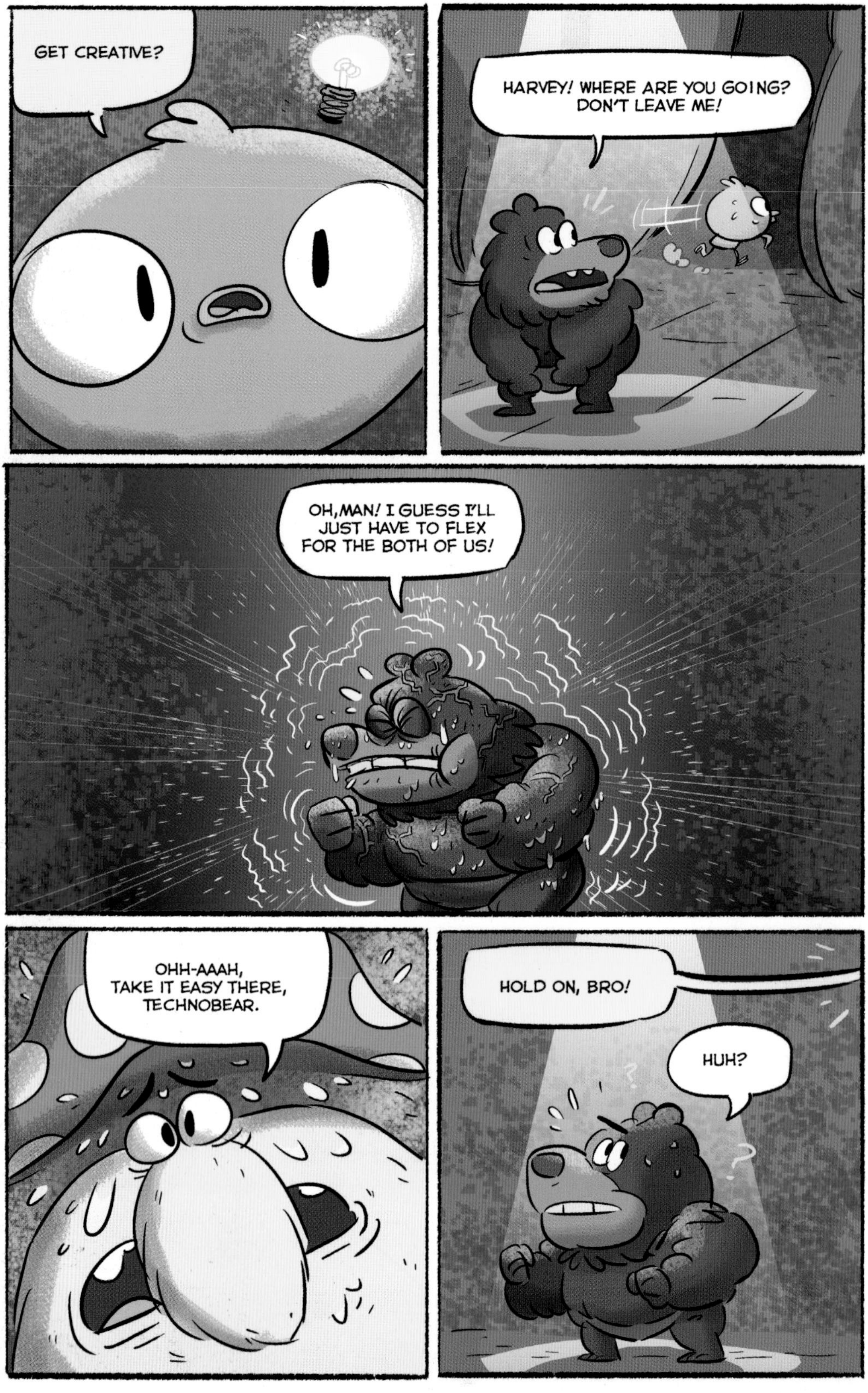
GET CREATIVE?
HARVEY! WHERE ARE YOU GOING? DON'T LEAVE ME!
OH, MAN! I GUESS I'LL JUST HAVE TO FLEX FOR THE BOTH OF US!
OHH-AAAH, TAKE IT EASY THERE, TECHNOBEAR.
HOLD ON, BRO!
HUH?

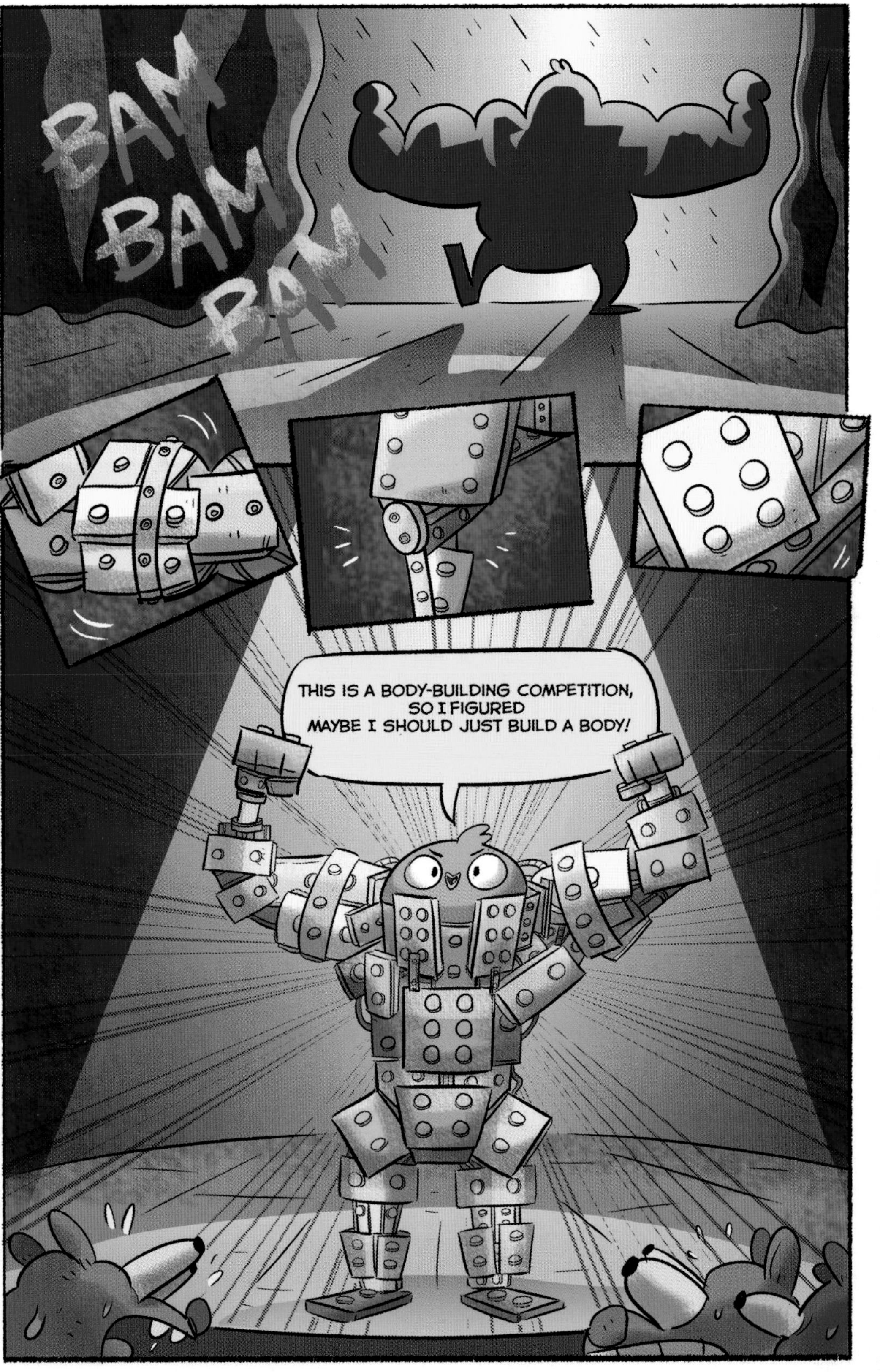
BAM BAM BAM
THIS IS A BODY-BUILDING COMPETITION, SO I FIGURED MAYBE I SHOULD JUST BUILD A BODY!

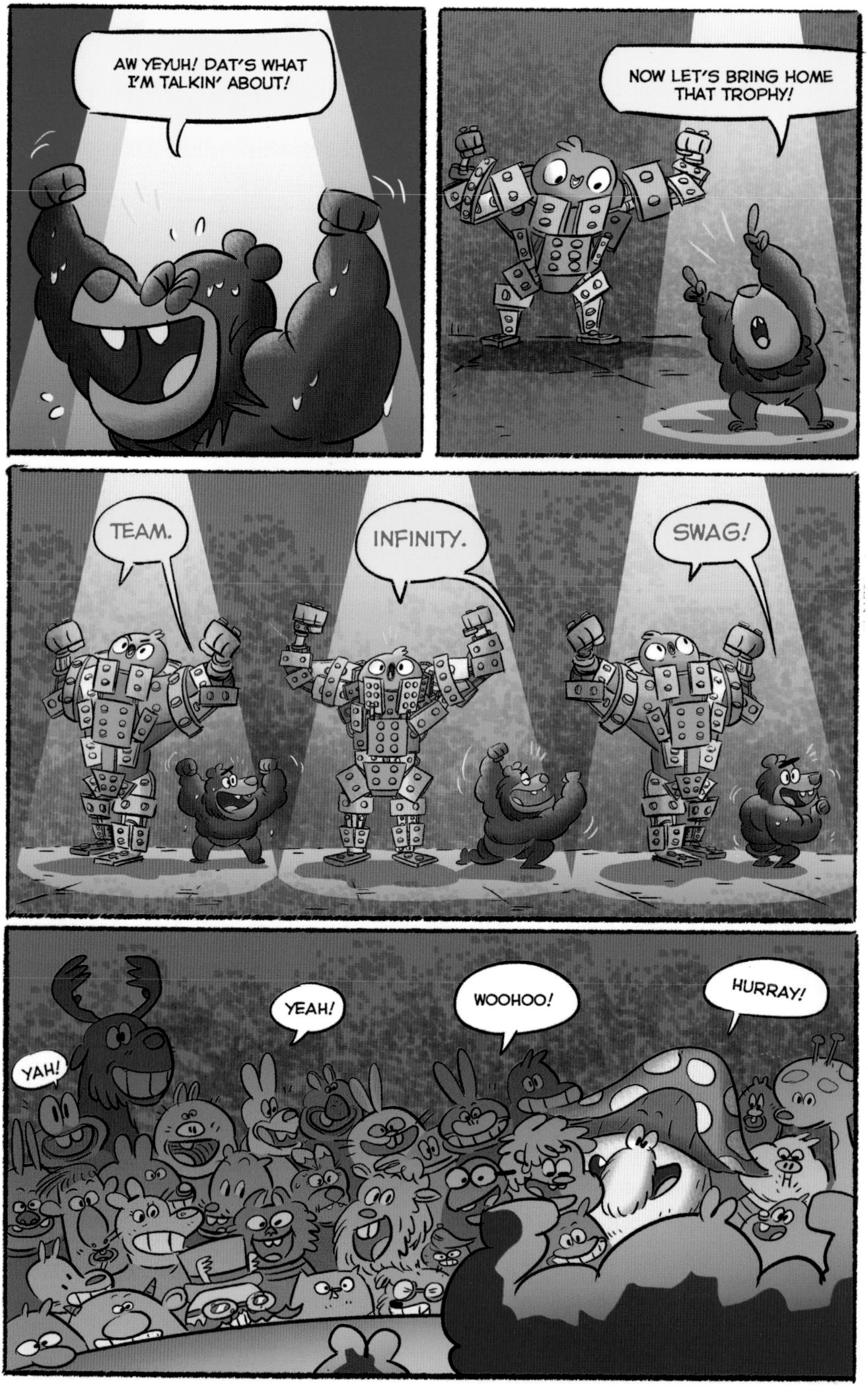
AW YEYUH! DAT'S WHAT I'M TALKIN' ABOUT!
NOW LET'S BRING HOME THAT TROPHY!
TEAM.
INFINITY.
SWAG!
YAH!
YEAH!
WOOHOO!
HURRAY!

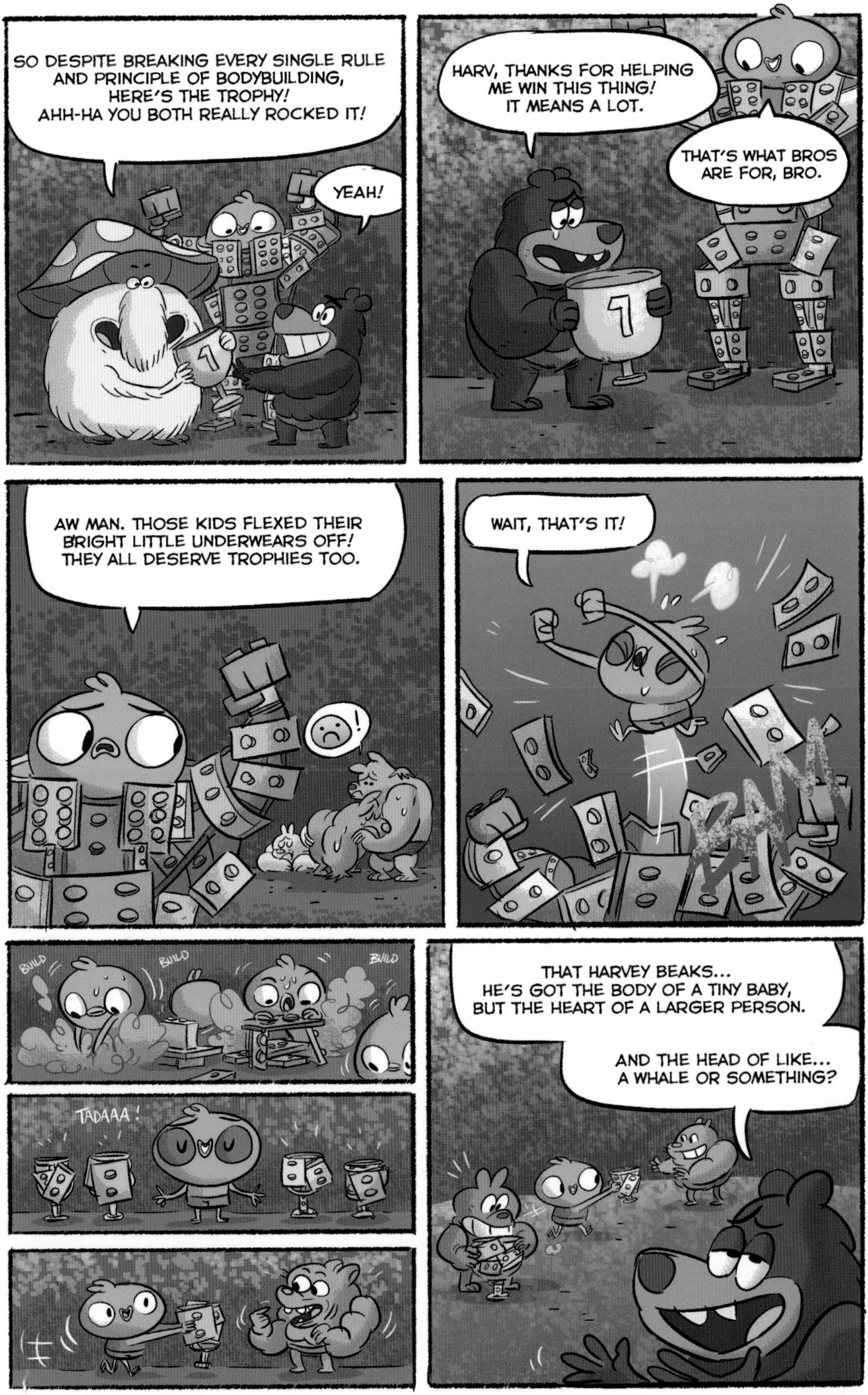
SO DESPITE BREAKING EVERY SINGLE RULE AND PRINCIPLE OF BODYBUILDING, HERE'S THE TROPHY! AHH-HA YOU BOTH REALLY ROCKED IT!
YEAH!
HARV, THANKS FOR HELPING ME WIN THIS THING! IT MEANS A LOT.
THAT'S WHAT BROS ARE FOR, BRO.
AW MAN. THOSE KIDS FLEXED THEIR BRIGHT LITTLE UNDERWEARS OFF! THEY ALL DESERVE TROPHIES TOO.
!
WAIT, THAT'S IT!
BAM
BUILD
BUILD
BUILD
TADAAA!
THAT HARVEY BEAKS... HE'S GOT THE BODY OF A TINY BABY, BUT THE HEART OF A LARGER PERSON.
AND THE HEAD OF LIKE... A WHALE OR SOMETHING?

END

WATCH OUT FOR PAPERCUTZ™

Welcome to fun-seeking, forest-friendly first HARVEY BEAKS graphic novel from Papercutz—those cuddly critters dedicated to publishing great graphic novels for all ages. I'm Jim Salicrup, the city-dwelling Editor-in-Chief, and I'm here to take you behind-the-scenes at Papercutz...

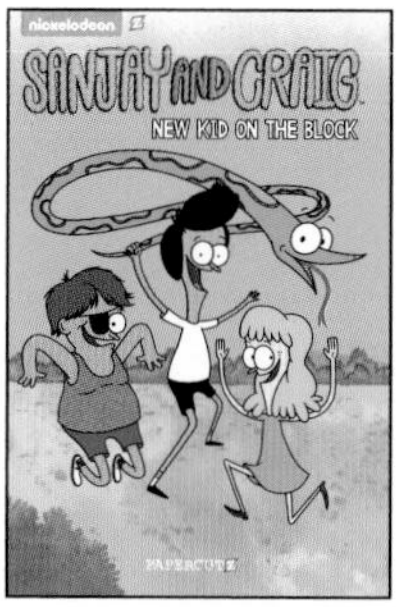

nickelodeon
SANJAY AND CRAIG
NEW KID ON THE BLOCK
PAPERCUTZ

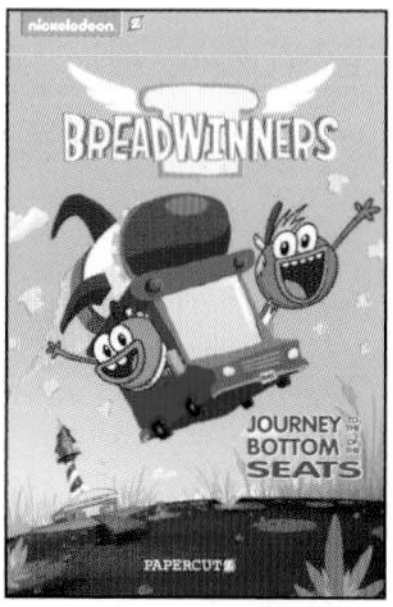

nickelodeon
BREADWINNERS
JOURNEY
BOTTOM
SEATS
PAPERCUTZ

If you've picked up either the SANJAY AND CRAIG or BREADWINNERS graphic novels, you already know most of this. But for those of you just hopping on the Papercutz bandwagon, here's the story of how these graphic novels came to be. A little over ten years ago, Papercutz publisher Terry Nantier and I founded this little comicbook company to address a need—there just didn't seem to be enough comics and graphic novels for kids. That was incredibly ironic, since most folks think of comics as being for kids. After ten years of producing all types of comics for all ages, we made an incredible deal with the awesome folks at Nickelodeon to create a line of graphic novels based on their latest and greatest new animated series. This really is a match made in cartoon heaven -- Nickelodeon, loved my millions of kids for their brilliant cartoon shows and characters, and Papercutz, the graphic novel publisher devoted to creating the best comics for kids—together at last!

Terry and I, along with Joan Hilty and Linda Lee, got to spend a day at the Nickelodeon Animation Studio where we talked about our plans with the creators of Sanjay and Craig, Breadwinners, Harvey Beaks, and more. Everyone was excited and as thrilled as we were about the characters leaping off the TV screen and onto the comicbook page!

To kick off this historic publishing partnership, we launched an all-new NICKELODEON MAGAZINE, which in addition to features such as posters, activities, calendars, etc., is jam-packed with comics—the very same comics we'll be collecting in our graphic novels. The magazine is available wherever magazines are sold, and is also available by subscription. Just go to papercutz.com/nickmag for all the details.

Editors Michael Petranek and Suzannah Rowntree helped get the comics started, but the bulk of the editorial work was handled by Bethany Bryan (Associate Editor/Papercutz) and Joan Hilty (Comics Editor/Nickelodeon). Together, working with writer Stefan Petrucha, Carson Montgomery, Shane Houghton, artist Andreas Schuster, and colorists Laurie E. Smith and Matt Herms, they've come up with the HARVEY BEAKS graphic novel you see before you.

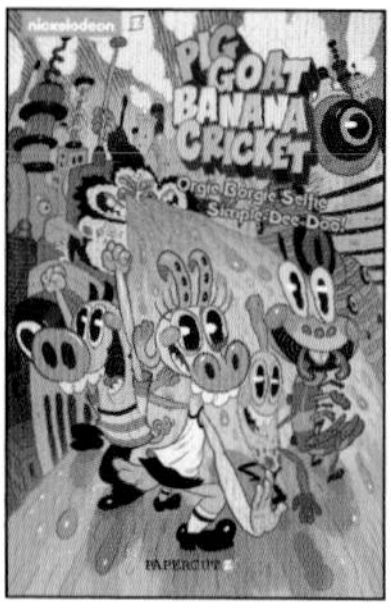

nickelodeon
PIG GOAT BANANA CRICKET
PAPERCUTZ

But this is just the beginning! Coming up next will be the debut of the first PIG GOAT BANANA CRICKET graphic novel! Is this the Nickelodeon Age of graphic novels or what? And the best part is that you are a BIG part of it! Tell us what you think of what we're doing—you're opinion matters to us. Our goal is to produce graphic novels that you will love as much as the original TV shows. Write to us at the addresses below and tell us if we succeeded or not. We'll be waiting for your comments!

Thanks,

Jim

STAY IN TOUCH!

EMAIL:	salicrup@papercutz.com
WEB:	papercutz.com
TWITTER:	@papercutzgn
FACEBOOK:	PAPERCUTZGRAPHICNOVELS
FANMAIL:	Papercutz, 160 Broadway, Suite 700, East Wing, New York, NY 10038

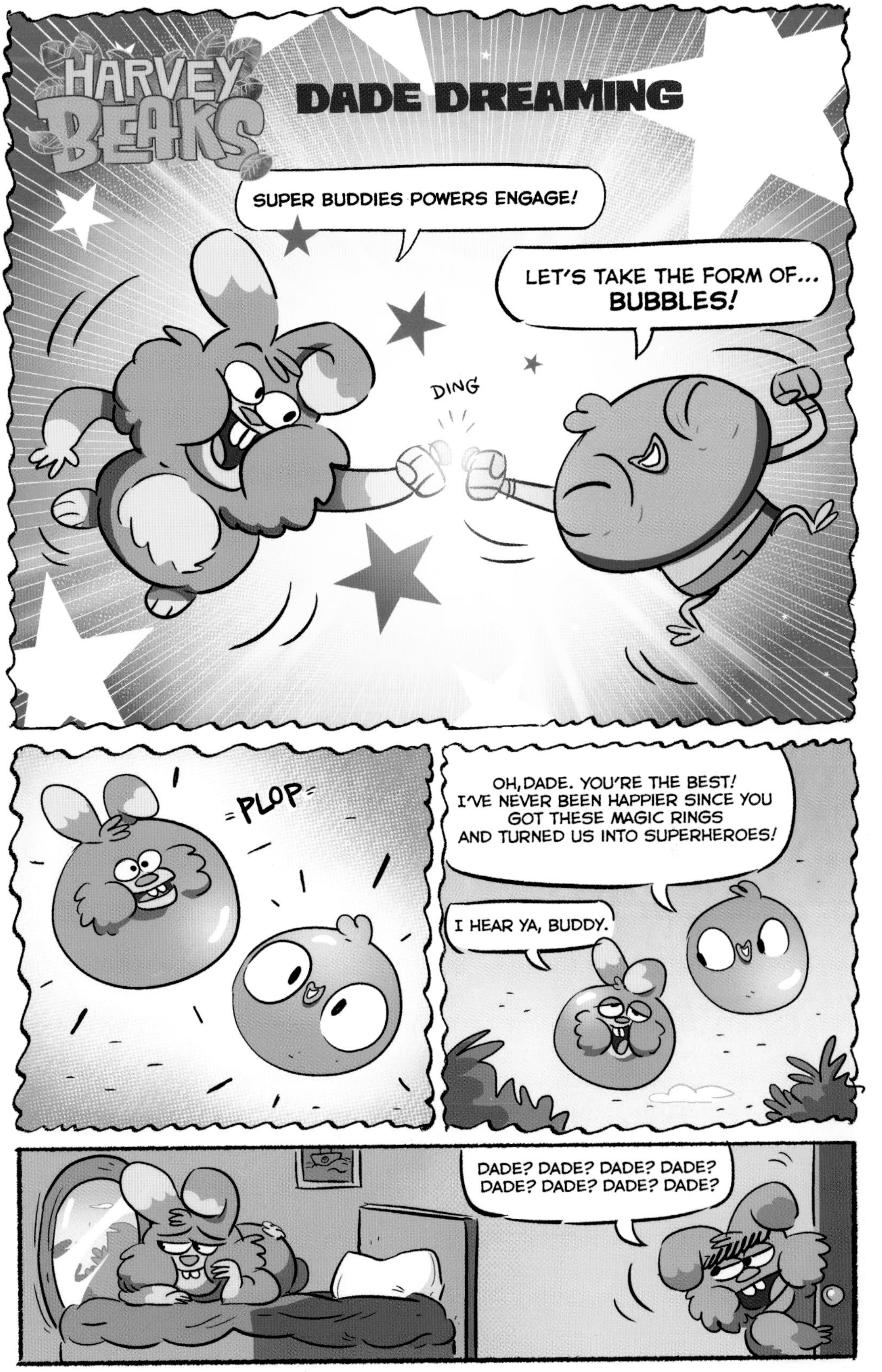
HARVEY BEAKS
DADE DREAMING
SUPER BUDDIES POWERS ENGAGE!
LET'S TAKE THE FORM OF... BUBBLES!
DING
PLOP
OH, DADE. YOU'RE THE BEST! I'VE NEVER BEEN HAPPIER SINCE YOU GOT THESE MAGIC RINGS AND TURNED US INTO SUPERHEROES!
I HEAR YA, BUDDY.
DADE? DADE? DADE? DADE? DADE? DADE? DADE? DADE?

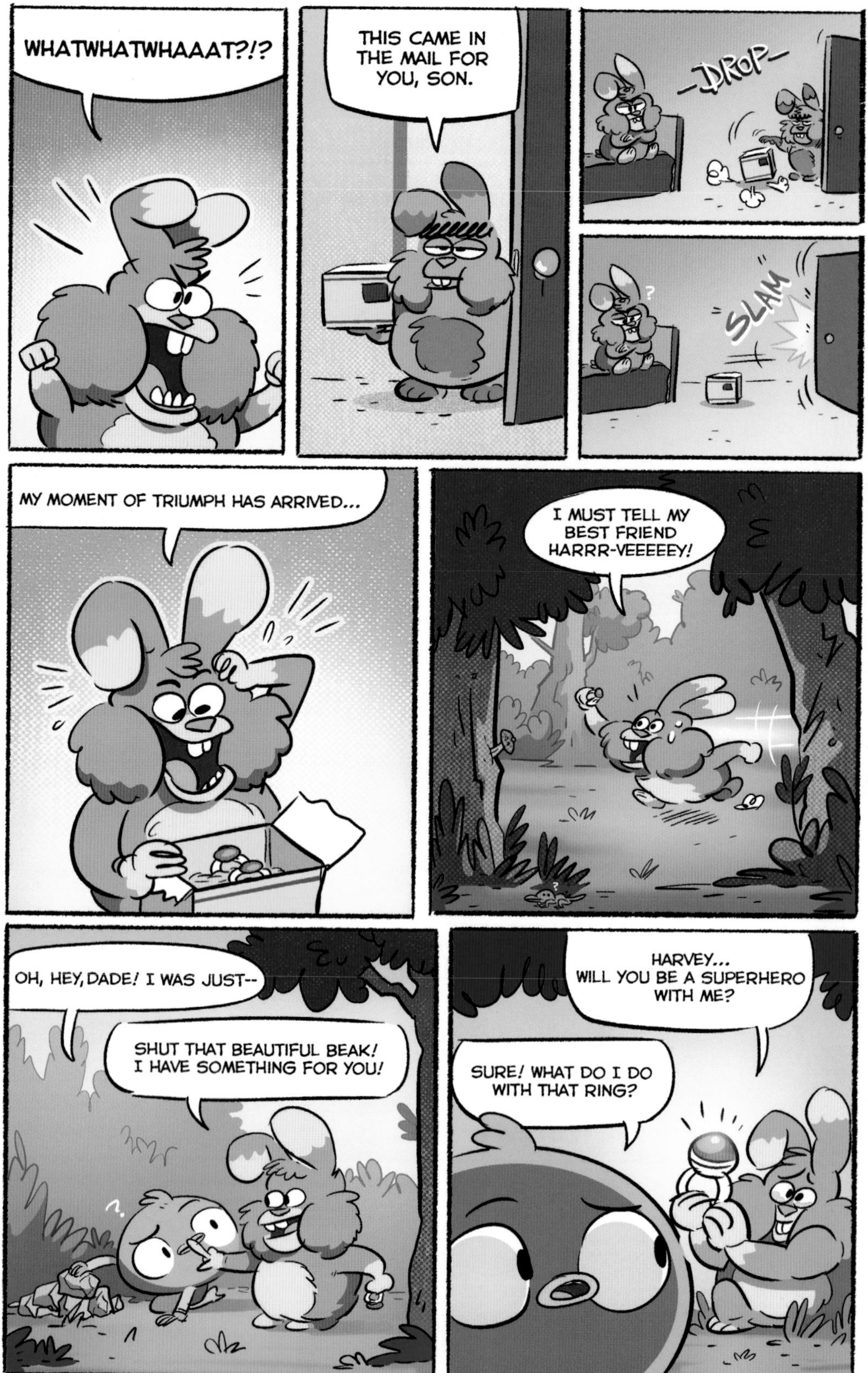
WHATWHATWHAAAT?!?
THIS CAME IN THE MAIL FOR YOU, SON.
-DROP-
SLAM
MY MOMENT OF TRIUMPH HAS ARRIVED...
I MUST TELL MY BEST FRIEND HARRR-VEEEEEY!
OH, HEY, DADE! I WAS JUST--
SHUT THAT BEAUTIFUL BEAK! I HAVE SOMETHING FOR YOU!
HARVEY... WILL YOU BE A SUPERHERO WITH ME?
SURE! WHAT DO I DO WITH THAT RING?

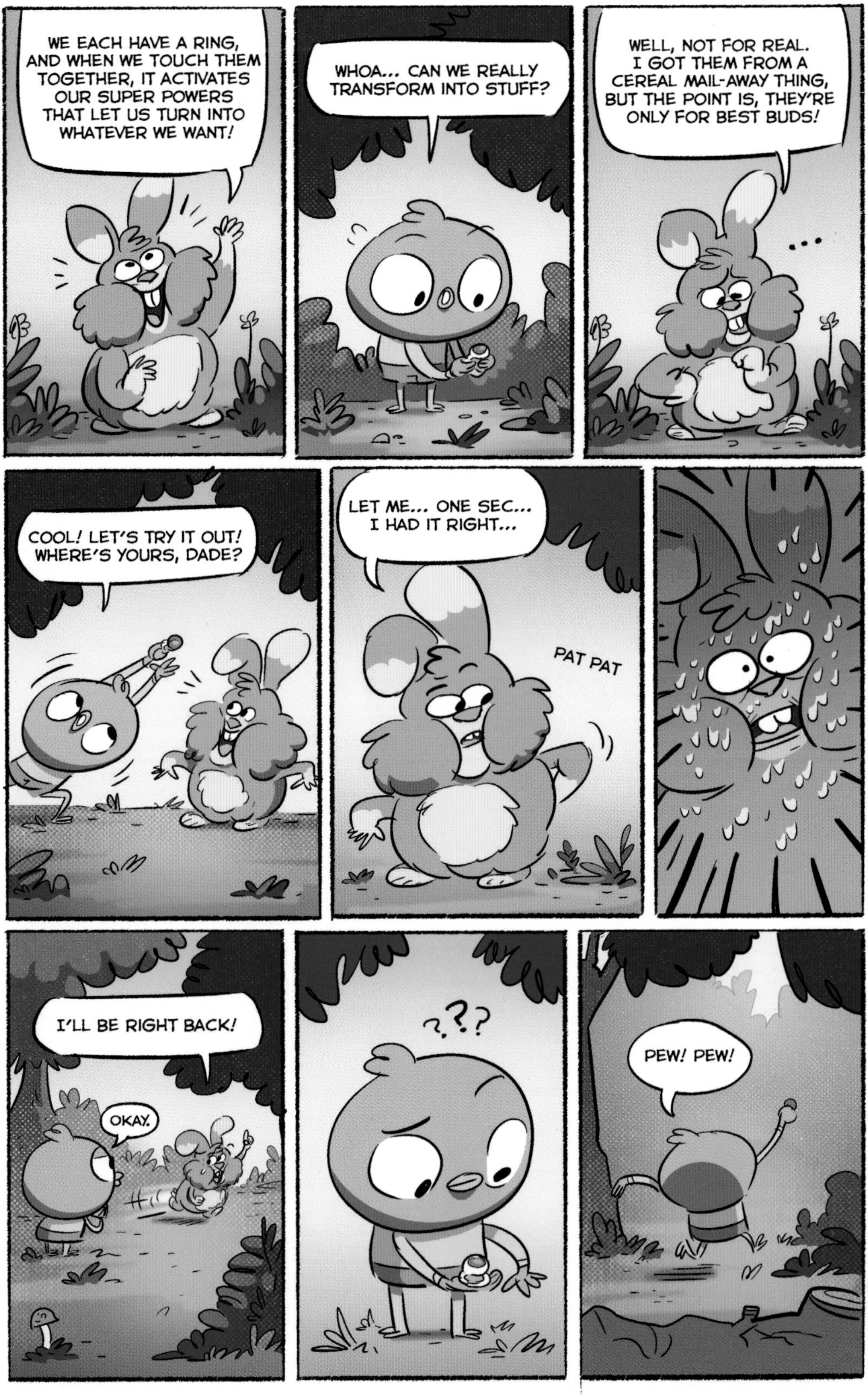
WE EACH HAVE A RING, AND WHEN WE TOUCH THEM TOGETHER, IT ACTIVATES OUR SUPER POWERS THAT LET US TURN INTO WHATEVER WE WANT!
WHOA... CAN WE REALLY TRANSFORM INTO STUFF?
WELL, NOT FOR REAL. I GOT THEM FROM A CEREAL MAIL-AWAY THING, BUT THE POINT IS, THEY'RE ONLY FOR BEST BUDS!
...
COOL! LET'S TRY IT OUT! WHERE'S YOURS, DADE?
LET ME... ONE SEC... I HAD IT RIGHT...
PAT PAT
I'LL BE RIGHT BACK!
OKAY.
???
PEW! PEW!

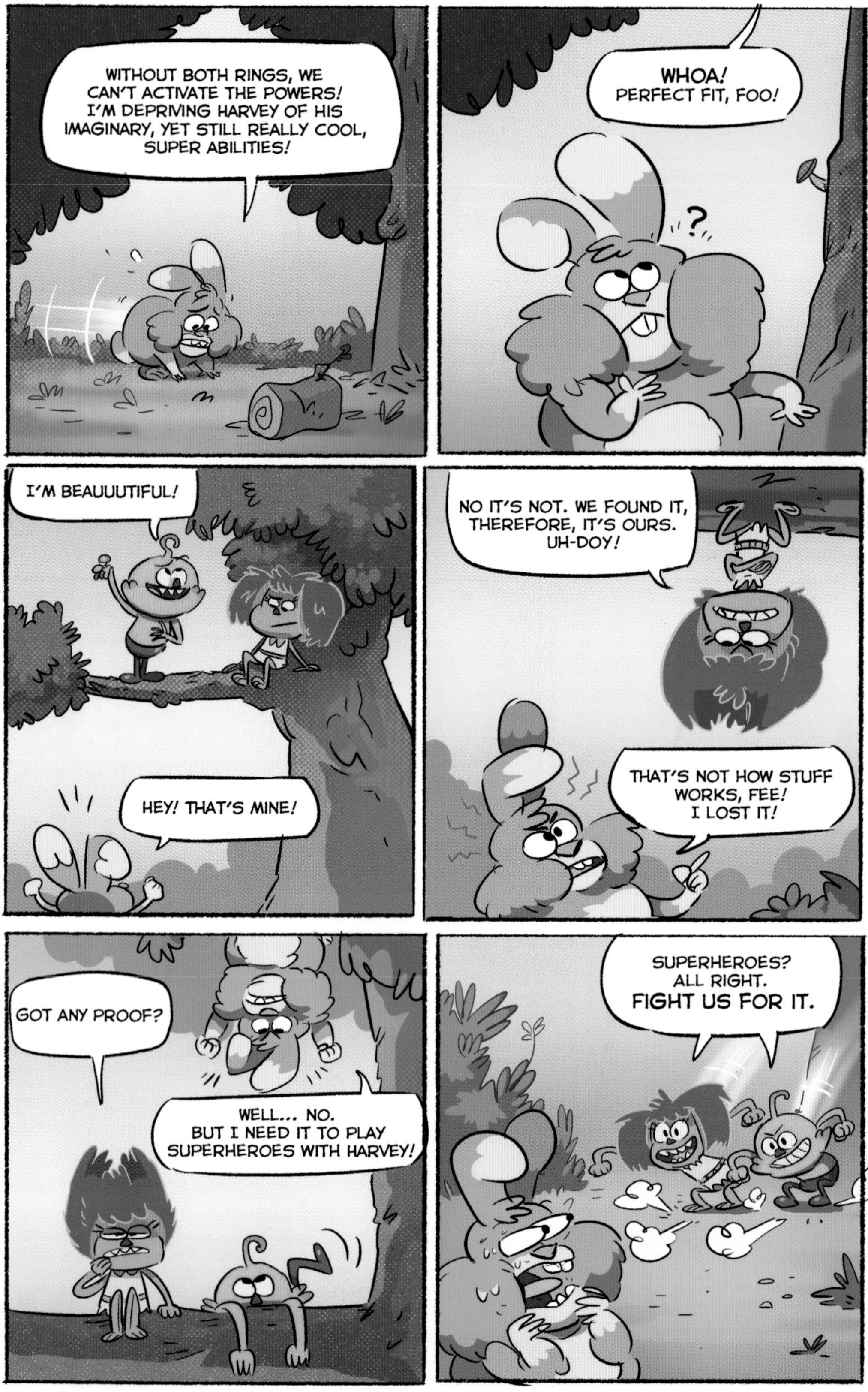
WITHOUT BOTH RINGS, WE CAN'T ACTIVATE THE POWERS! I'M DEPRIVING HARVEY OF HIS IMAGINARY, YET STILL REALLY COOL, SUPER ABILITIES!
WHOA! PERFECT FIT, FOO!
?
I'M BEAUUUTIFUL!
HEY! THAT'S MINE!
NO IT'S NOT. WE FOUND IT, THEREFORE, IT'S OURS. UH-DOY!
THAT'S NOT HOW STUFF WORKS, FEE! I LOST IT!
GOT ANY PROOF?
WELL... NO. BUT I NEED IT TO PLAY SUPERHEROES WITH HARVEY!
SUPERHEROES? ALL RIGHT. FIGHT US FOR IT.

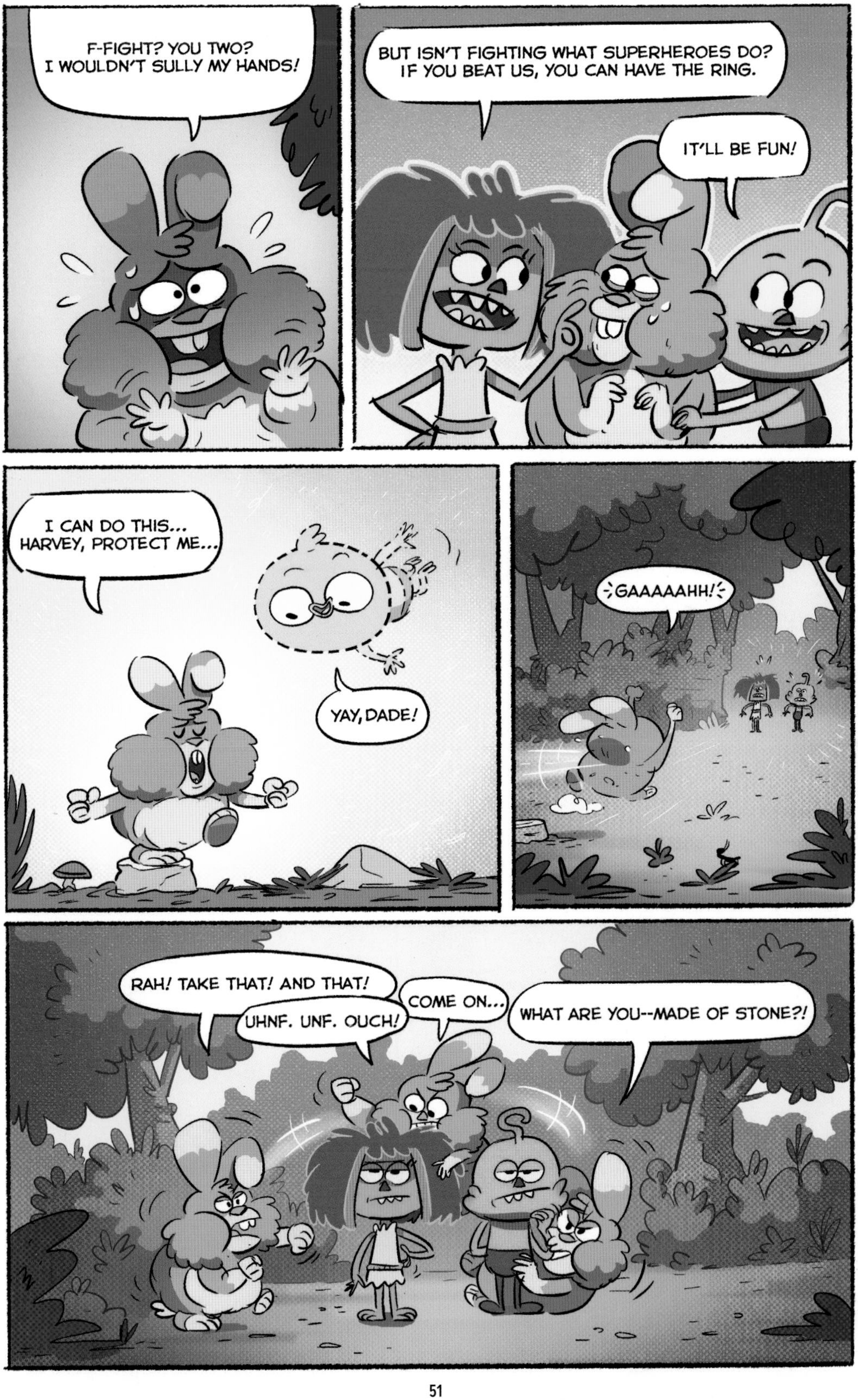

F-FIGHT? YOU TWO?
I WOULDN'T SULLY MY HANDS!
BUT ISN'T FIGHTING WHAT SUPERHEROES DO?
IF YOU BEAT US, YOU CAN HAVE THE RING.
IT'LL BE FUN!
I CAN DO THIS...
HARVEY, PROTECT ME...
YAY, DADE!
GAAAAAHH!
RAH! TAKE THAT! AND THAT!
UHNF. UNF. OUCH!
COME ON...
WHAT ARE YOU--MADE OF STONE?!

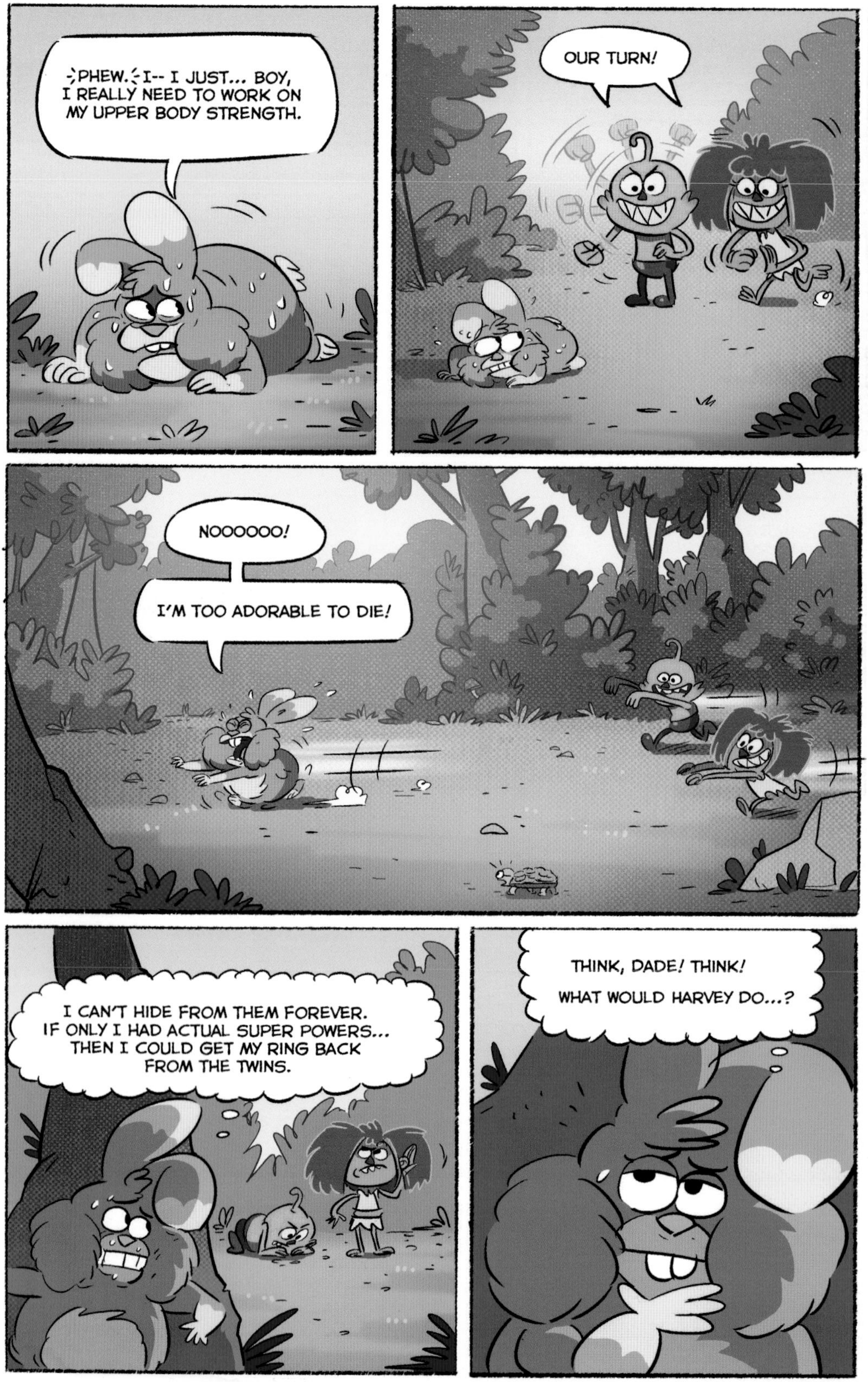
PHEW. I-- I JUST... BOY, I REALLY NEED TO WORK ON MY UPPER BODY STRENGTH.
OUR TURN!
NOOOOOO!
I'M TOO ADORABLE TO DIE!
I CAN'T HIDE FROM THEM FOREVER. IF ONLY I HAD ACTUAL SUPER POWERS... THEN I COULD GET MY RING BACK FROM THE TWINS.
THINK, DADE! THINK!
WHAT WOULD HARVEY DO...?

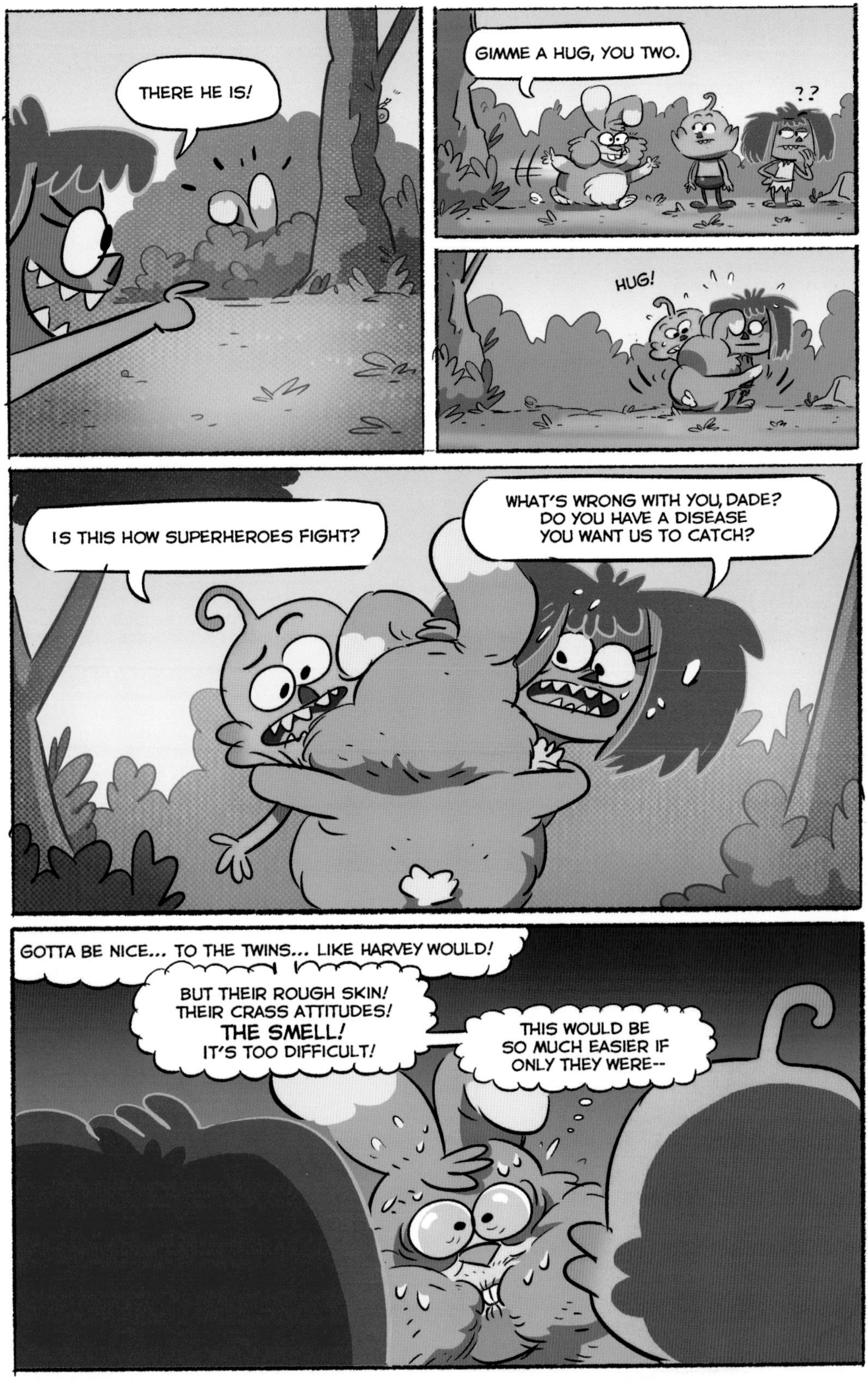
THERE HE IS!
GIMME A HUG, YOU TWO.
??
HUG!
IS THIS HOW SUPERHEROES FIGHT?
WHAT'S WRONG WITH YOU, DADE? DO YOU HAVE A DISEASE YOU WANT US TO CATCH?
GOTTA BE NICE... TO THE TWINS... LIKE HARVEY WOULD!
BUT THEIR ROUGH SKIN! THEIR CRASS ATTITUDES! THE SMELL! IT'S TOO DIFFICULT!
THIS WOULD BE SO MUCH EASIER IF ONLY THEY WERE--

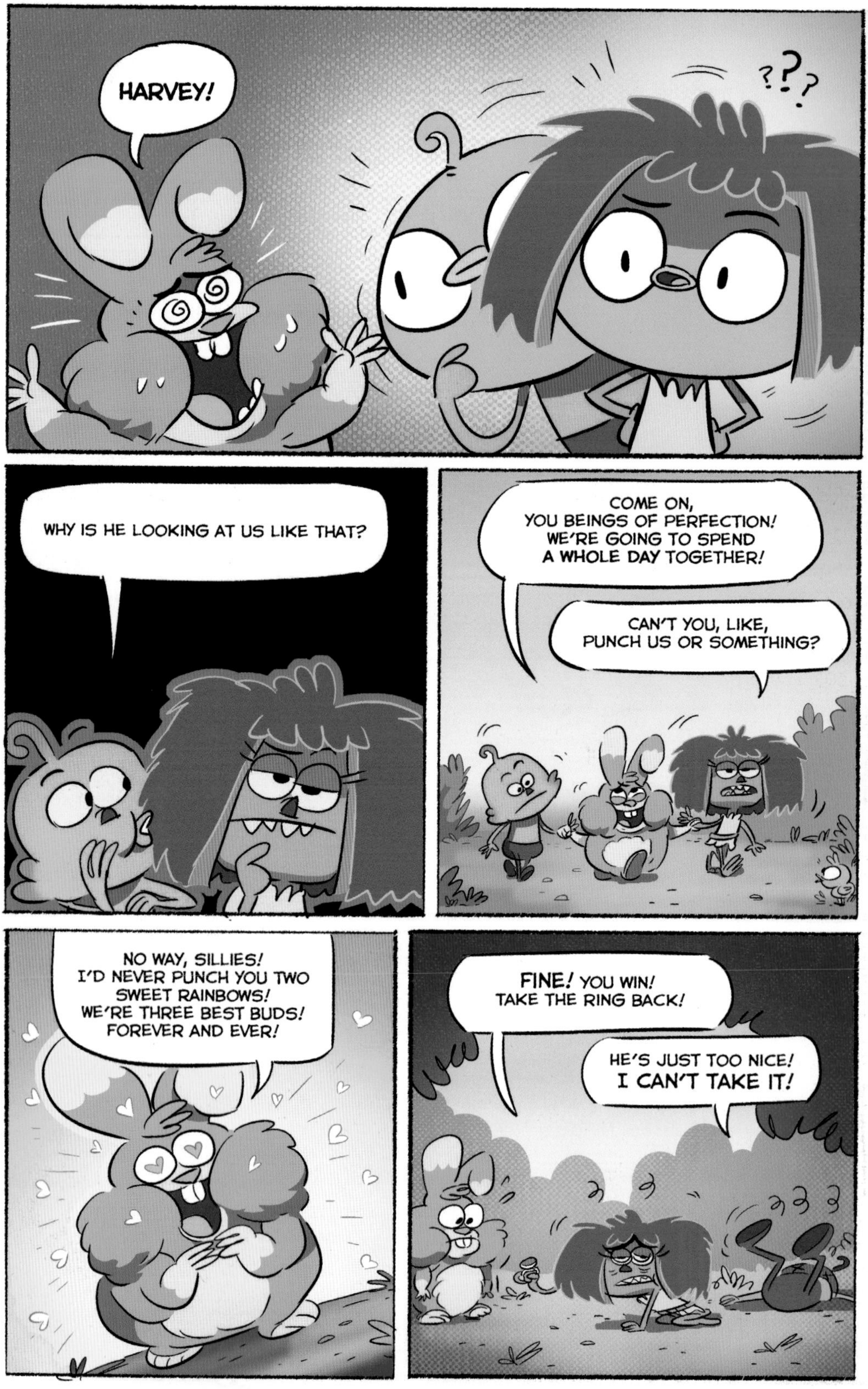
HARVEY!
???
WHY IS HE LOOKING AT US LIKE THAT?
COME ON, YOU BEINGS OF PERFECTION! WE'RE GOING TO SPEND A WHOLE DAY TOGETHER!
CAN'T YOU, LIKE, PUNCH US OR SOMETHING?
NO WAY, SILLIES! I'D NEVER PUNCH YOU TWO SWEET RAINBOWS! WE'RE THREE BEST BUDS! FOREVER AND EVER!
FINE! YOU WIN! TAKE THE RING BACK!
HE'S JUST TOO NICE! I CAN'T TAKE IT!

RUN, FOO! RUN!

BUT...
TWO HARVEYS...

OH, RIGHT! THE REAL HARVEY!

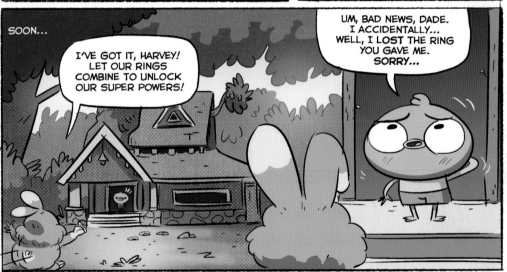

SOON...

I'VE GOT IT, HARVEY! LET OUR RINGS COMBINE TO UNLOCK OUR SUPER POWERS!

UM, BAD NEWS, DADE. I ACCIDENTALLY... WELL, I LOST THE RING YOU GAVE ME. SORRY...

BUT I DO HAVE A **SURPRISE** FOR YOU.

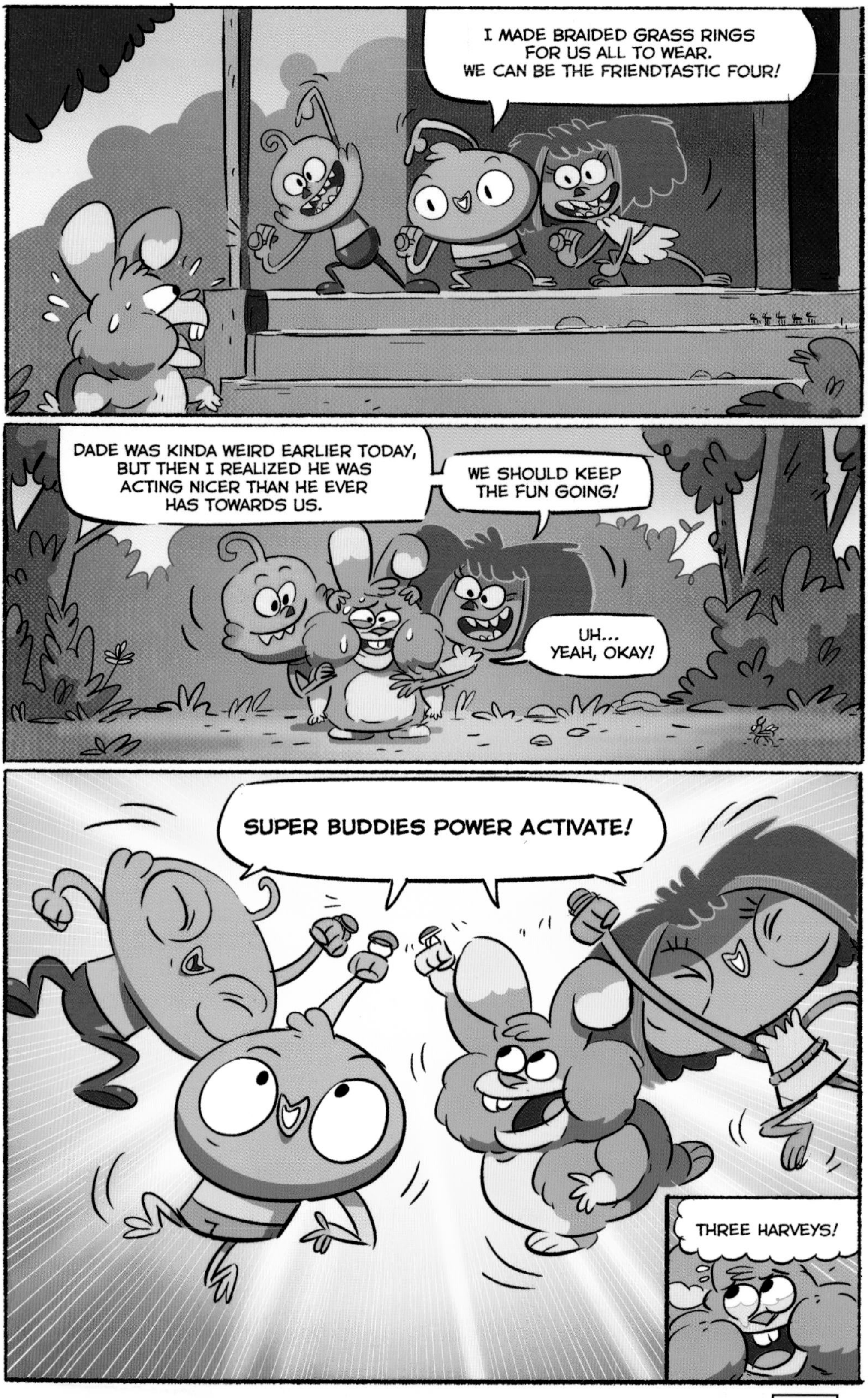
I MADE BRAIDED GRASS RINGS FOR US ALL TO WEAR. WE CAN BE THE FRIENDTASTIC FOUR!
DADE WAS KINDA WEIRD EARLIER TODAY, BUT THEN I REALIZED HE WAS ACTING NICER THAN HE EVER HAS TOWARDS US.
WE SHOULD KEEP THE FUN GOING!
UH... YEAH, OKAY!
SUPER BUDDIES POWER ACTIVATE!
THREE HARVEYS!

END